MY WARRIOR WOLVES

My Warrior Wolves

SANCTUARY, TEXAS BOOK FIVE

KRYSTAL SHANNAN

Copyright © 2016

This is a work of fiction. Names, characters, places, and incidents either are the product of the author's imagination or are used fictitiously, and any resemblance of fictional characters to actual persons living or dead, business establishments, events, or locales is entirely coincidental.

All rights reserved. No part of this book may be used or reproduced in any manner without written permission from the author and publisher except in the case of brief quotations embodied in critical articles or reviews, or within the sharing guidelines at a legitimate library or bookseller.

Please do not participate in or encourage piracy of copyrighted materials in violation of the author's rights. Purchase only authorized editions.

WARNING: The unauthorized reproduction, sharing, or distribution of this copyrighted work is illegal. Criminal copyright infringement, including infringement without monetary gain, is investigated by the FBI (http://www.fbi.gov/ipr/) and is punishable by up to five years in a federal prison and a fine of $250,000.

This book contains content that is not suitable for readers 17 and under.

Published by KS Publishing

Formatting by Kate Tilton's Author Services, LLC

(www.katetilton.com)

ACKNOWLEDGMENTS

I'm so excited for you to get to read Travis and Garrett and Charlie's story. The world of Sanctuary has grown so much since I started with My Viking Vampire. It's amazing how the characters have come to life in my mind and on paper. I hope you feel the same way. There are still so many stories to tell and villains to fight. I hope you enjoy this journey with me.

A huge thanks to all the people who help make these books come together. My cover artist, my editors, Fiona and Jacy, my fantastic publishing assistant who makes my life so much easier - Annie you're amazing!

Also, a huge shout out to the wonderful fans in Krystal's Cavalry! You rock and I love you all and I hope that you know how much I appreciate the time you take out of your busy lives spend with my books.

Last but never least, my amazing husband and daughter who put up with Mama being part cyborg and always being connected to either the laptop, the iPad, or my phone. I do everything for you and because of you both. I love you both so dearly. You are my life. Thank you for putting up with my crazy.

CHAPTER ONE

GARRETT

A huff escaped from between my lips as I slid onto an empty barstool at Riley's. The ache in my chest had turned from an annoying throb to the pounding of a fatal wound. If not for the Lycan moral code, I'd already be hauling ass up to Ada to bring Charlie down to Sanctuary, kicking and screaming if necessary. Her feelings on the matter could be discussed later. She should be with us. Somehow, we had to make her see that. Being away from her slowly ate away pieces of my soul. The scent of her heat clung to my brother and I. No amount of cold showers would relieve the need that hardened my dick every time I thought about her, either.

I couldn't believe she'd sent Travis and I both away. We'd risked our lives. Saved her from Xerxes' clutches in Savannah. Yet she'd sent us packing with no regard to the developing magickal bond torturing all three of us. There was no way she wasn't hurting either. Once a mate bond started growing, only death would snap the connection.

My brother, Travis, sat next to me and waved to the tall redhead at the far end of the bar. Riley Moore acted as pack liaison between Rose, the town of Sanctuary's leader and founder, and the rest of the Lycans in town. It helped keep the peace, and most of us tried to avoid Rose anyway... except when the cafe served really good food. Which tended to be more often than not.

"What's happening, boys?" Riley asked, setting a pair of freshly filled beer steins in front of us. "You look like you swallowed a rattlesnake and it's trying to come back up, Garrett. What's eating you?"

"Nothing." I hoped she would accept the answer and just leave, but Riley didn't budge. In fact, she plopped her elbows on the bar and leaned forward, balancing her chin on her laced-together fingers.

"That's a bunch of bullshit." Her gaze flitted toward my brother. "You don't look much better, hon," she said to Travis. "I hear you left someone both of you want up in Ada."

"Who told you, Riley?"

"People talk," she said, winking. "This is a bar. Nothing stays secret for long when it stumbles in here."

I growled and took a long swig of the dark amber liquid in front of me. The rich brew hit just the right spot, and I closed my eyes for a second.

"Pretty good, right?" Riley asked. "One of the pixies over at the market grew me some extra special barley. This new recipe has been the favorite all week."

"It's really good," Travis answered before I could speak.

I nodded, agreeing with my older brother.

"I saw Eira's tattoo the other day. Gorgeous work as usual. Who wants to take credit?"

Travis shook his head.

I raised my mug and nodded. "That woman is something else. Despite how vampires normally react to silver, she barely flinched once from the silver needle."

"Probably has something to do with the fact that she's over a thousand years old and a Viking shield maiden." Riley tipped her head to the side. "She seems like a nice addition to the town, along with Killían. She's--what?--protector number six?"

"Yep."

"Y'all staying for the news brief at five? It's supposed to be from the SECR today. Not sure what those bastards have to share, but I've got to watch it anyway. Just in case there's something to report to Rose. The Sentinel never sleeps, you know."

"Nothing on the radio tonight?" Travis asked her, setting his half-empty beer stein on the countertop.

She shook her head. "Nope. Nothing scheduled."

I rotated the barstool until I could see the large screen TV she had on the wall just to our right.

She produced a remote control from beneath the bar and pressed a few buttons. The screen blared to life. News reporters stood in front of the federal building in downtown Savannah where Charlie said they'd been held in cages in the basement. The footage was old, at least several days. Politicians and the military fed exactly the information they wanted the people to see, but every once in a while, it did offer up something useful.

I half expected to see Xerxes on screen, but he wasn't that confident...or he just didn't have enough control of the SECR Republic yet to risk being exposed for the murdering bastard that he was.

Instead, a man with a teen girl standing just behind him flashed across the screen for a moment. The male spouted some garbage about how the SECR no longer had to live in fear of Others. That they had purged their homeland and the creatures were gone.

The political bullshit didn't interest me, but the Asian-looking teenager standing behind the Mayor of Savannah did. Not unusual in and of herself, she looked eerily like the Kitsune woman who'd come back from Savannah with the rescue party only a short week ago. And she looked drugged –her body supported completely by a large bodyguard.

"Do you see what I do?" I whispered under my breath.

"Yep. Calling Mikjáll," Travis answered, pulling his cell phone from his pocket. "Take a pic when they show her face again."

I nodded and jumped up from the seat. Walking forward, I raised my cell and snapped a couple shots.

"They are on their way over."

"Who is it?" Riley asked. "You know that footage was taken several days ago, right?"

Nodding my head, I climbed back onto the barstool. "Yeah, I know. Not sure who she is exactly, but she looks too much like Riza to be a coincidence."

"The Kitsune female living with Mikjáll?"

"Yep. That would be her. That dragon barely leaves her and the baby's side." I turned back to the TV for a moment, but the Mayor was gone, and now some General prattled on about how new security measures were being implemented over the course of the next few weeks. Mostly just a bunch of bullshit that reminded people who lived in the SECR that it was illegal to own a firearm unless they were part of the Republic's military force.

Riza, barely five feet tall, came into the bar, followed closely by the seven-foot hulking Drakonae male. One wrong move on the dragon's part could send the fox shifter flying into the wall. For a man as big as Mikjáll, he managed to move with an unnatural fluidity.

He and Riza made an atypical match to say the least.

Riza should've been terrified of the angry dragon who'd come to Sanctuary having just lost his wife and his home. Instead, she'd latched onto him, and to everyone's surprise, he connected with her. They were inseparable. Both sympathetic to the other's losses.

I'd been worried about having Mikjáll on the mission to Savannah, but he'd proved he could keep his cool… for the most part. He had transformed into a fire-breathing dragon in the middle of a Savannah street, risking his species to exposure, but every single one of us knew we were alive because of that choice.

"Where is she?" Riza barreled straight toward the TV screen, but not seeing what she expected, she turned to my brother and me. "Mikjáll said you saw a girl who looked like me."

I pulled my phone from my pocket and swiped the

screen until the picture I'd taken showed. She plucked the device from my hand and covered her mouth as a semi-hysterical sob escaped her lips.

"She's alive! I thought they killed her. We were captured together, but separated nearly a year ago. They told me she died."

"Who?" Mikjáll asked, stepping up to look at the picture. "Is she family?"

Riza nodded.

By this time, the entire bar had fallen into a hush. Even the Lycans in the back room playing pool had stilled.

"It's my sister. We were there together in Savannah. Djinn kidnapped us from our home. One day she became very ill, and they took her out of the facility where they were keeping me. The morning after they took her, one of the nurses told me Sochi died."

The tears streaming down the young woman's face made me wish I could disappear. "I shut down for months. I'm not even sure how long. They had to force feed me. They gave me shots, tried to artificially inseminate me at least four times before it finally took. Once I realized I was pregnant, I started eating again. I couldn't hurt her. But then as the pregnancy continued, I realized they meant to take the baby away from me."

"The next day, I used the powers I'd told them I didn't possess and slipped away while they were cleaning my room."

"How did you slip a guard?"

Riza's skin shimmered, and she literally disappeared from view. I could smell her presence. She hadn't left the room, but I couldn't see her. A second later, something glimmered a few feet away and she reappeared.

"Impressive," I said. "Wouldn't mind having that ability myself."

She nodded. "I wandered that facility for days after that, at term and miserable, scrimping and stealing food to stay alive. I birthed Suki in a closet and was nearly caught the next morning when I slept too long."

"Fuck!" Travis snarled, only to receive an angry glare from the hovering Drakonae.

"Several days later, I stumbled on the group of Lycans making their escape. I followed them out of the building and then met your rescue party. If Mikjáll hadn't grabbed me and Suki off the street that night, I don't know where we would be." She leaned into Mikjáll's large form, and the Drakonae wrapped an arm possessively around her shoulders. "We have to get her out of there. Now."

"We?" I asked, grimacing. "*We* barely made it out of Savannah alive the first time. What makes you think going back again will be any better? Plus, that video is a few days old. She might not be there anymore."

"I have to go back for her," Riza said, her eyes swirling with a mixture of pearlized colors. Sparks of electricity arced from her fingertips, a more offensive ability Kitsune possessed, and I couldn't help an instinctual flinch. No one ever wanted to be electrocuted. "Surely someone will help me. We can't just leave her there."

The appearance of the Kitsune's sister was likely a trap, but the pleading in her voice tugged at my heart, but the only person who might know a safe way in and out of the SECR didn't want to have anything to do with me or my brother. Charlie'd told us to leave. Even though the mate bond between us had started forming, we'd honored her wishes. The ball was in her court. We wouldn't approach her again unless she asked for us. It wasn't the Lycan way.

CHAPTER TWO

CHARLIE

"This is my pack!" I snarled, slapping my palm on the countertop of the large island in the lodge's kitchen. How dare my uncle and cousin make a play for alpha.

"You're not part of a bonded pair, Charlie. You can't lead us. This pack has been through hell, and half of them are buried on a hillside near the Vicksburg Bridge." My uncle's brown eyes narrowed, but I could see the darkness slowly claiming his soul. Yes, the pack had been through hell. I'd fucking lost my parents in Savannah. Xerxes killed them right in front of me. If not for Manda distracting him, he most certainly would've raped and killed me the same night.

I hated her for betraying the pack, but I owed the double-crossing Djinn bitch my life. Not just for that, but also for breaking us out of the prison we'd been locked up in.

On top of everything, I'd sent away the only two people that could bring any peace to my traitorous body. Travis and Garrett were my mates. I knew that. But a triad mating was rare among Lycans.

Wolves didn't typically share well.

Travis and Garrett didn't seem concerned about the *sharing* aspect, and I craved them both, but at the same time, I worried how the pack would react to me bonding with two. They would expect infighting and jealousy. They would see us as weaker when, in fact, our magick would be amplified because of the extra point of the triad. But I had to put that aside for now.

I'd been prepared to leave the Mason pack. To desert the lodge in Ada all together, but after losing my parents, I couldn't...I wouldn't leave. My needs came second to the pack. That responsibility trumped the burning desire that raged through my body. No matter how much I wanted a family and to settle down away from the chaos of sneaking in and out of the other Republics to save Lycans who couldn't get out, I absolutely would not leave the fate of my family to my uncle and my idiot of a cousin.

One problem at a time –right now, I needed a united pack.

I could figure out how to have my family later.

"My parents just died, Uncle Victor," I said, lowering the tone of my voice. "You will not start this right now. This pack needs to heal. It's barely been a week." I was the alpha heir, bonded or not. He owed me respect. They all owed me that much.

Drawing in a deep breath, I tried to calm the rage

simmering in my blood. But every nerve sparked, and my skin burned. My heat cycle demanded fulfillment. Fulfillment I was actively denying myself. In the midst of all this fighting with my uncle and cousin, every thought always circled back to Travis and Garrett. The hunger for my Fated mates had not quieted. Only my sheer determination to care for my pack got me through each day without them.

I had been right to send them away... at least, I thought I had.

"That is exactly why I'm doing this." My uncle's voice dropped to match my angry tone, and I could hear the threatening rumble deep in his chest.

Asshole. He'd always been jealous of my father's position as pack alpha—his brother.

I rolled my neck to the left and then to the right, enjoying the pop as my vertebrae realigned. More people filed into the kitchen, some older, some younger, but my eyes flew to my cousin. He'd lost his father at Vicksburg, my father's youngest brother. Dean had always been mostly friendly, but his gaze at that moment put ice in my veins.

They were all turning against me. I tried to do what was best for the pack, but they didn't care. Worse, instead of thinking logically to solve the political upheaval in my home, all I could focus on was how much my body ached and throbbed and wanted desperately to be fucked by the two men I'd told to go home so I could grieve with my family and attempt to put the pieces of the pack that were left back together.

Except no one let me grieve. Not for a second.

Everyone wanted something. And I had nothing left to give. If my parents had survived, I'd already be gone. If it were one of the other more seasoned males vying for the alpha position –anyone but my uncle –I would already be gone. But it wasn't. And I was stuck. My parents would've expected me to do everything in my power to keep their legacy going. I wouldn't disappoint them.

"You're in heat, Charlie. But you haven't made a move on anyone in the pack," Dean said slowly, moving closer to the front of the crowd. "If you were truly invested in this pack, you would've already bonded with the male that triggered it. Instead, you show weakness by trying to lead by yourself. Lycan packs must have a pair."

My uncle's lips curved into a smile that made my palms sweat. They really were going to try and steal the pack from me.

"Why don't you just step aside and let the male heirs decide who's going to step up for this pack?" Dean asked, flashing a dark look at our uncle.

Damn. Not only were they both trying to shove me out of my rightful place, they were going to fight each other. Either one of them as alpha for this pack would be chaos.

Uncle Victor was a power-hungry asshole who would use the pack to further his needs. While my cousin Dean was only twenty-five years old, a baby in comparison to my eighty years of experience in the jacked-up place formerly known as the United States. He just didn't have a clue.

He wouldn't continue the smuggling runs. Neither of them would, and that mission had driven my parents since the Riots. The pack had been founded on helping trapped families. All of that would disappear if I lost control. I didn't want to continue the rescues either, but my parents would turn in their graves if I didn't. So I would continue on the path they'd set for the pack.

If I called Travis and Garrett, they would just tell me to leave. Tell me to come back to Sanctuary and live with them and abandon the pack that didn't think I could lead without a male at my side.

Though tempting, I'd be lying to myself if I denied I'd considered the possibility. But abandoning my parent's legacy wasn't what I'd promised them a few minutes before they'd been murdered by that fucking psychopathic lunatic, Xerxes.

My fate was sealed. I stayed with the pack no matter what.

I remembered life before the Riots of '46. It'd been easy. Lycans took everything for granted. Our kind had become complacent and careless. We paid for it and brought all of humanity down on our backs and on a handful of other supernatural races in the process.

Tap. Tap. Tap. I turned. Kara, now a single mother of two little ones, stood in the kitchen doorway. Her husband had died in the massacre at Vicksburg Bridge. She approached slowly, her gaze darting between my uncle, my cousin, and me.

"There's... there's a man at the door who says he has a message from Xerxes."

"What!" Bile rose in my throat, burning through the top layer of skin, making me grimace. I lunged for the hallway, but my uncle grabbed my upper arm before I slipped away.

"Stay calm and hear him out, Charlie. He's got a valid point to make."

I shoved away from him and shuddered. "What the fuck, Uncle Victor? You invite the enemy literally to our doorstep and you want me to *stay calm*?"

"It's time for things to change," Dean said, stepping up to stand next to me. His six-foot-eight frame made me overwhelmingly aware of how much smaller I was compared to either of them.

If it came down to it, I didn't have a chance in hell of winning this fight without help.

I wanted time to consider my options.

Time to grieve.

Time to let the pack heal from the losses we'd suffered before I tried to fight with Travis and Garrett about staying here. And we would fight.

I already knew they didn't want to stay in Ada.

But there was no time left. If I didn't call them, I might lose the pack forever.

CHAPTER
THREE

TRAVIS

"Charlie is the only one left in Ada who could help, but..."

"I know," Riza said. "But this is my sister. I won't leave her. She would go back for me."

"What about your baby, Riza? You can't go crawling around a military state when the biggest badass on the planet is searching for you," I said, crossing my arms resolutely over my chest. It was ridiculous. The idea of that little female fighting any *regular-sized* person was amusing.

She pulled away from Mikjáll and reached for my arm. A few seconds later, a jolt of electricity arced from her fingertips into my skin. *Holy shit.* I'd never come so close to biting my tongue clean off.

"I'm perfectly capable. I just need a little assistance," she answered, her voice dark and filled with a determination that reminded me of Charlie. This little fox was ready to dive into the henhouse.

Her electric display didn't convince me she was ready to deal with hens that bit back. We needed Charlie, or at least one person from the pack, to guide us. They knew all the back ways in and out; without that, we would easy targets.

"Give us a little time, Riza. Let me make some calls," Mikjáll said. "I assure you, we will get your sister back. I will personally make sure of it."

The little female visibly relaxed against Mikjáll's body. A surge of jealousy heated my body, and I clenched my hands into fists. He better not expect us to contact Charlie. She'd made it clear that we weren't welcome in Ada without her permission. Neither of us would cross the line she'd drawn. No male Lycan would disrespect a female who'd said *no*.

"We can't ask the pack in Ada," I said slowly, waiting for the Drakonae to get pissed and lash out. He didn't, though.

"I didn't think we could. They took a terrible hit. But there are people here who might help. Would it be too much to ask you to reach out to Charlie and ask what route would be our best option? She would have more knowledge of the least patrolled highways than anyone in town."

Maybe. It was possible we could get away with a harmless question like that. But I wasn't putting it past her to ignore our call completely. I'd left my cellphone with her so that she could contact us —just in case she changed her mind. It'd been enchanted by Meredith Bateman, one of Sanctuary's resident witches, so the signal couldn't be tapped or traced by any government.

Garrett's phone buzzed on the bar top behind us. The face of the glass lit up, and my name flashed on the screen. I reached for the device, but Garrett was quicker.

"Charlotte?" he asked, using her full name.

In my mind, she was Charlie—tough, badass, a survivor who fought for what she wanted. But hearing him use Charlotte reminded me that, just because she had hard edges, I couldn't forget that she had a softer side as well —even if she'd forgotten.

His voice softened, and my heart raced, listening for her response. Why had she called? Was something wrong?

"I have a problem, and I need you two to help me."

I could hear her voice perfectly though she was on the other side of the line.

"We will be there in a few hours," Garrett shot back, glancing at me. His eyes reflected my worries. Something was really going to hell if she was asking us to come to Ada. She knew we wanted her. And that we wanted her to come back to Sanctuary with us. We both ran the tattoo shop now and couldn't imagine leaving the friends --- make that family--- we had here.

"This doesn't mean I'm changing my mind about leaving, but an uncle and one of my cousins allowed a Lycan loyal to Xerxes into my living room. I'm upstairs right now, but I have to go talk to this asshole..."

Her voice faded away, laced with fear and uncertainty.

Just the fact that she made the phone call was a huge step for us. It gave us another chance to try and seal the mating bond. But the call also meant she was desperate. I hated that she had to feel so lost before she sought us out.

"Do your best to stall, Charlotte," Garrett said. "We are coming."

"Thank you," she whispered before the line went dead.

"Sounds like she's having a crisis up there," Mikjáll said.

"We leave in twenty. I'm sorry, Riza."

The female shook her head. "She's your mate. I understand. We will find others here to help find my sister, right?" Riza asked, tipping her head up to meet Mikjáll's gaze.

"Yes, we will, my dear." Rose's calm voice carried across the still-quiet bar. "Boys, I expect you to do whatever is necessary to help your mate."

I nodded, surprised to see Rose in Riley's bar. It wasn't often that she left the cafe. She lived above her restaurant and rarely left the center of town.

"Mikjáll, take Riza, go get the baby, and take them both to the Castle. They need to be under guard while you are not at her side. I'll make a few calls and meet you outside the cafe." The small Persian woman turned to the Kitsune female. "Do you know why Xerxes wanted your baby?" Riza shook her head and frowned. "The blood of a Kitsune infant can transfer its abilities."

"What do you mean?" I asked, taking a step toward the group and motioning to my brother to stop.

Rose looked at me for a moment, the wisdom and pain of millennia weighing her down. She turned to

Riza and spoke again. "Xerxes is trying to mask his DNA."

"How do you know Xerxes still has Riza's sister?" Mikjáll interrupted. "The video showed her with the Governor of the SECR."

"He wants power. The only way he can get more is to convince the human population he's one of them. The Washington Republic has been developing scanning technology for years. It only makes sense that he has her."

My stomach threatened to crawl up my esophagus. *Scanners.* At least at the moment we had a fighting chance to hide and avoid detection, but if scanning tech was implemented across the Republics, it would only be a matter of time before it was installed on satellites. "He's preparing for a move on the WR, isn't he?"

Rose nodded. "Him allowing Sochi on the news is a lure. Our only advantage is that Riza and her baby are safe in Sanctuary. They must stay here. We need to get her sister out of there before..." Rose cut herself off and frowned.

"What?" Riza begged. "What is he going to do to my little sister? She's sixteen! You said only an infant's blood was useful to him. He can't use her unless—" A sob wrenched from her tiny body, and Mikjáll caught her before she collapsed to the ground. "Please help her, please! You have to get her back!"

"We will, Riza," Rose spoke calmly, reaching forward to touch Riza's arm. "I promise we will get her back." Rose turned to face me again and nodded. "Go to your mate. We will help Riza. And I am coming, too."

My heart hurt for the Kitsune, but Rose knew Garrett and I needed to get to Charlie. Still, I was shocked Rose was willing to leave Sanctuary to go after this young girl.

"Thank you, Rose."

CHAPTER FOUR

CHARLIE

Voices filtered up the stairs as I made my way down into the living room. The scent of strangers was thick in the air, mixed with arrogance and disgust.

I rounded the corner and entered the great room of the lodge.

Uncle Victor sat in one of the high wing-back chairs in front of the fireplace. Dean stood behind him with a smug look on his face that made me want to pummel him. An unfamiliar Lycan male sat on the couch, flanked by two more unfamiliar Lycan males, both dressed in full body armor. Thoughts of strangling my uncle and cousin on the spot danced through my head.

"You had no right to invite them into our home without my permission." My voice was cold, calculated, and—I could only hope—pissed enough to get my attitude across quickly. "I am the pack alpha until the *pack* tells me otherwise."

"I think you've made quite enough decisions for this pack, Charlotte," Victor growled. "You need to listen to Martin. He comes with a peace offering from Xerxes. Don't you think this pack has seen enough pain and suffering for a lifetime?"

"Get out!" I glared at the stranger on the couch. "Get out of my home. Now!"

"I think you should hear me out, Charlotte. Don't you think the pack deserves to have peace?" The stranger stood and held up his hands as if he were surrendering. But that was the furthest thing from his mind; I could smell the arrogance coming off of him and his companions.

Why couldn't Victor and Dean smell the lies? Were they so terrified of fighting for a just cause that they would surrender to my parents' murderer? Could they really be this blind?

I snarled, struggling to hold back the wolf inside that wanted nothing more than to rip his throat out. My vision changed, and I knew my eyes were bright yellow. How dare he have the audacity to waltz into my home after what Xerxes did!

Moving slowly, I approached him until I was barely a foot away. He was taller than me, but I didn't care. I tilted my chin up at the traitorous bastard and growled.

"I watched him brutally stab my mother and slice her throat open in front of me. He enjoyed it. He teased my father as he gutted my mother in front of us both." My gaze swung to my uncle, and I saw the slightest hint of guilt, maybe even remorse. "Then he killed my father." A sob slipped out. The memories of that horrid night filled my mind. If not for Manda distracting him, I would've died that night, too. He would've killed me, and Manda had known he wouldn't kill her.

But Manda had wanted to die. She'd hoped for it.

She'd thrown herself into the Phoenix's fire. After risking everything to get us out, she still tried to end her life. It was her fault half the pack was dead, but if it hadn't been for her... I'd be dead.

"War has casualties, Miss Mason," he replied, his tone flippant and uncaring. "Xerxes is offering your pack peace. They merely have to serve him when needed and pledge loyalty to my alpha. Join my pack and your lives will cease to be torture. He will stop hunting you." He glanced around the room and then looked back to me. "All of you."

My mouth ached, and I mentally pushed my wolf back. She wanted his blood... any blood as retribution. But it wasn't the right time. This bastard likely had dozens more soldiers with him waiting in the shadows. Our numbers were so low.

I needed help. I hated that feeling.

My parents told me after the Riots I would one day lead the pack. Every decision I made would be scrutinized. And they were. My choices had brought me to this crossroad.

This next choice would not only define my life, but the life of everyone in the pack that looked to me as their leader in the absence of my parents.

I glanced past the emissary into the hallway and saw one of the now-single females standing silently, watching. Several other moms stood behind her. All of them had lost their husbands and mates.

"Gina," I said, gesturing to the youngest woman in the front of the hall. "Would you and the other ladies please show our guests into the kitchen? I need to speak to Victor and Dean alone."

She nodded and went into the main room.

I turned to the emissary and his two thugs and motioned them to follow the women. "Please, excuse me. But I need to speak privately with my pack about your proposal."

The traitorous scum smirked, and it took everything inside me not to lunge at him. They followed Gina and the others out of the main room, disappearing down another hallway that led into the lodge's huge kitchen.

Turning my focus back to my uncle and cousin, I released the growl I'd been holding back.

"Dad's office. Now." I stormed out of the room and didn't turn around again until I was on the other side of my father's large office and fortified behind his massive mahogany desk.

My uncle perused the room, and his gaze lingered on my father's desk chair. Great significance rested with that chair. Leaders sat there. Alphas. Even though I wasn't seated, I had taken my position behind the desk, leaving him and Dean on the other side.

"Charlie. This is what's best for the pack. We don't have the resources to keep doing..."

"What? To keep helping our people? People Xerxes also slaughters if they don't agree to his terms."

"To be a Lamassu's bitch." Victor's lip curled, and his dark eyes briefly flashed yellow.

I scoffed. "I'd rather be Rose's bitch than yours. Tell me you're not stupid enough to believe that lying asshole, Uncle."

"He's offering us a way out, cousin," Dean spoke up. "I'm with Uncle Victor. My father would still be alive, as well as yours, if we didn't send pack into the SECR again and again and again. The smuggling has to stop. We can't keep sacrificing lives for everyone."

"So who deserves to live, Dean? Who gets to choose? You're telling me you want Xerxes to have that right. To have the right to choose whether we live or die. We will be at his beck and call, just like the asshole in our kitchen."

"Hush, Charlie. You know he can hear you," Victor said, raising his hand to shush me. "You're being unreasonable. My brother and your mother fought the good fight, and they paid the ultimate price for their choices. You almost did, too. Don't you want a chance to live without all of this?"

"That's just the point. You can't get away from this!" I waved my hands around the room. "*This* is never going to change if you capitulate to his demands. At least my parents had the balls to fight for their species' right to survive. You just want us to beg for scraps."

"Better to beg sometimes, Charlie, than to starve," Victor answered, narrowing his eyes.

Coldness swept through me, and I knew I'd lost them

both. Dean was young and male, and he would do anything his uncle said was right. The only reason I had an opinion Victor couldn't manipulate was because I was old enough to see through his bullshit.

"I am alpha by right of blood. What that traitor out there proposes...what you would have me support is voluntary slavery. My parents would've said it's better to fight through hell than willingly give up your freedom. Are you both such cowards that you would tuck your tails between your legs and beg for your lives, hoping he doesn't run out of ways you can be useful to him?"

My uncle scoffed. "It's an alliance. Not slavery. He is one being." *I'm quite sure that's what Manda and the rest of the Djinn believed at first, too.* "And you aren't bonded. Without a male at your side, you're no more fit to lead this pack than a—"

"Choose your words carefully, Uncle. This is my pack by right. You are challenging me."

"Oh, I am. We'll see how far your right of blood gets you when you have no pack willing to follow you."

I shook my head. "The pack won't go for this." They were being ludicrous. Xerxes wouldn't stop with this. There would be concession after concession, and that was only if he didn't kill us all anyway after my uncle agreed to the terms.

I focused my gaze on Dean. What was his role in this takeover?

"Dean, are you going to fight Victor for alpha, too? Work together to force me out then turn on each other?" I narrowed my gaze and smirked. "How long do you think you'll last? You may both have a bonded mate, but neither of you have the pack's interest at heart. You're just cowards. Where are your mates now? Why aren't they standing beside you?" I let my voice rise. At this point, I didn't care. They'd both turned on me, and I needed them to focus on each other instead.

At least until Travis and Garrett got here.

CHAPTER FIVE

GARRETT

Travis tossed his bag into the back of the black SUV and climbed in next to me. We didn't usually use personal vehicles to and from Ada, but there was no time to arrange transport on one of Harrison Bateman's buses. Instead, we'd be relying on Mikjáll's thermal vision to alert us to local police or military convoys that wouldn't appreciate the speed at which we planned to travel down the highway.

Another black SUV pulled out from the alley beside the diner. Rose was driving, and Mikjáll, who still hadn't mastered twenty-first century motor vehicles yet, rode copilot. The thousand-year-old Drakonae could shift from a seven-foot tall man into a scary-as-hell, fire-breathing creature the size of a small department store, and yet he couldn't grasp the simple concept of 'sharing' the road with other drivers.

There were several other figures in the van. I could

hear their heartbeats, but the tinted windows prevented identification.

"Do you know who else is with them?"

"Calliope, Alek, and Jared."

"Calliope?" I frowned. "What possessed her to volunteer for a black ops mission?"

Travis smiled. "You don't know Calliope very well, little brother."

"She makes clothes. She's a siren..."

He chuckled again, and I couldn't help the irritated growl that vibrated in my chest. We shouldn't be bringing another woman along. I knew Rose was more than capable. But Calliope...?

"If you think Rose is frighteningly powerful, Garrett, you've never seen a Siren angry. Calliope may be a creature of lore who lured sailors to their deaths in ancient Greece, but she's one you don't ever want to piss off."

Their SUV built up speed as we made our way past a few buildings on the outskirts of Sanctuary. The highway was open and flat from here to Ada. I followed, increasing my speed to match theirs. Rose had insisted on making sure we made it to the Mason lodge house in Ada before continuing east to find and bring back Riza's sister.

Two hours into the drive, Rose's SUV slowed, and I followed suit, reaching the legally posted speed limit. We'd only passed a dozen or so cars the entire way and were always careful to stay on the less traveled, smaller interstates. A few moments later, we passed a parked TR patrol car, and I didn't relax until it was completely out of sight in my rearview mirror.

Mikjáll had seen them in time.

Hopefully, they wouldn't consider our two-car entourage suspect enough to follow. Being detained by the TR military or local police for any reason wasn't a quick process. They were thorough and made sure to dot every 'i' and cross every 't' for even the smallest offense. I doubted the bags of weapons and gear in the back seats of both vehicles would pass for unsuspicious behavior.

Five minutes later, we were flying down the highway again, the needle on the speedometer nudging the edge of 100 mph.

We continued, slowing when necessary and accelerating when possible. We trekked around the huge metroplex that was Dallas-Fort Worth. The two mega-cities had long since merged into one goliath metropolis. No one could really tell where one city or suburb started and the other ended anymore.

Soon the landscape turned back to rolling hills of grass and shrub trees. The old Oklahoma border didn't exist anymore; a dilapidated tourist center and what used to be called a rest stop flew past us as we crossed the bridge over the rusty water of the meandering Red River.

My heart sped a little faster as we continued up I-35. I glanced at my brother, and he nodded but didn't speak. We both needed to see her. The pull to return to her had been torture. But she'd asked us to leave, and a Lycan male never pushed for a mating that wasn't desired. The female held all the power in a courtship and could stop it at any point...for any reason.

She'd called, though. She'd asked us to come back. She needed our help.

My wolf pushed at my consciousness. It wanted to

howl in excitement and run in circles, but mostly I just wanted to get her horizontal on a bed and convince her to finish sealing the bond. When we'd left her, she'd been in full heat, and I could only imagine how her body had tortured her since we'd left. The heat cycle wouldn't stop until we bonded. She was punishing herself by keeping us away.

My brother and I had waited long enough. The thought of being in the same room with her again and not finishing the bond that pulled on all our souls made my lip curl and a growl vibrate in my chest.

"What?" my brother asked from the passenger seat.

I shook my head and shoved down my irritation. "Nothing. Just restless."

"You and me both. The first thing on the agenda, after giving the traitor Lycans an ass-kicking, is to lock the three of us in a bedroom and torture her with orgasms until she can't walk."

A laugh rippled through my body, shaking my chest. That certainly sounded like a good plan to me.

Both SUVs stopped in front of the Mason lodge just outside Ada's city limits. A shiny black Humvee was parked near the front of the lot, an obvious red flag compared to the old vans and battered sedans next to it. I shoved the stick into the park position and reached for the door handle.

"Stop."

I halted my hand and turned to face Travis. "What is

it?" We were both eager to see Charlie. What could possibly make him want to stall our reunion another nanosecond?

Then I heard them. Heartbeats east of the lodge, just over the ridge out of sight. A lot of heartbeats. Maybe fifteen or twenty. Slow. Still. Calculated.

They were soldiers, trained to be calm in every situation. A skill Travis and I both acquired during our long stints in the military.

"How did I miss it?"

Travis let out a sigh. "I did, too." He held up his cell phone, and a text message from Rose lit the screen.

Don't exit the vehicle. Soldiers on the east hillside.

I grinned. "Cheater."

"I think we're a little distracted at the moment," Travis admitted.

"I don't know about you, but I'm *A LOT* distracted at the moment. Is it just me or can you smell her from here?" I didn't think I was imagining it, but I'd been dreaming of her since walking away from the lodge weeks ago, and I could swear her scent filled the air now.

"I can, too. It's not just you."

The front door of the lodge opened. Three men exited, went down the front steps, and climbed into the Humvee. It drove off, pelting the nearby cars like a vengeful hailstorm.

A telltale vibration in Travis' pocket made me antsy. He pulled out his phone again and nodded. "Soldiers are moving away."

I looked at the other SUV. Mikjáll's door was open, and Rose's was, too. Yanking on my door handle, I shoved it wide and slipped from the large vehicle, closing the door gently behind me. No need to make a racket.

Travis rounded the hood, and we walked together toward the front of the lodge. Rose and Mikjáll fell into step behind us. The Phoenix and Gryphon stayed in the SUV, but their scent clung to Rose and Mikjáll's clothing.

"They don't want to come in?" I asked, glancing over my shoulder to the Sentinel of Sanctuary.

The petite, olive-skinned woman smiled and shook her head. "Guard duty. I wanted to speak with Charlie for a few minutes before we leave. Please give Mikjáll the keys to the SUV you drove. We will be taking both vehicles."

"No problem." I dug the keys out of my pocket and tossed them to the Drakonae.

CHAPTER SIX

CHARLIE

Footsteps on the patio made me jump. Was that damn wolf back with his cronies again? How many times today was I going to have to argue my case? It'd taken nearly two hours to get Victor and Dean out of my hair. Even now, I was pretty sure they were assembling a mutiny.

It's not like I could really blame them. These past weeks had been hell. There wasn't a Lycan in the pack who hadn't been affected by the massacre at Vicksburg Bridge.

A tap at the door drew me from my gut-twisting thoughts. Gina was standing in the doorway waiting for me to acknowledge her. At least common respect hadn't been completely lost already.

"We have company, Charlotte. People from Sanctuary, Texas."

I sucked in a breath. How had they gotten here this

fast? Glancing at the clock on the wall, I swallowed. It had been barely three hours. They had to have literally run out the door the second I called for help.

Shifting in my seat, I closed my eyes and focused on slowing my racing heart. The heat fever I'd learned how to suppress was rising up with the speed of an erupting volcano. Control was everything for an alpha, and I needed to remain in control.

Of everything.

Especially at this moment. Because if I didn't, my body would take what it wanted and leave the rest of me to clean up the mess afterward.

"Thank you, Gina. Would you show them into the office?"

She nodded and disappeared.

I stood from my father's chair behind the massive desk and walked to the window on my right. Two large black SUVs were parked outside, and if I wasn't mistaken, at least two or three people had remained inside one of them.

They're here! Their scent filled my lungs before they entered. Travis and Garrett were my mates. Fate hadn't changed her mind over the course of the time we'd been separated.

Boots clunked on the wooden floors, and my two Lycans walked in, followed closely by Mikjáll, the seven-foot-tall Drakonae dragon shifter. Behind him stood Rose.

Petite, beautiful, and more deadly than any supernatural being I'd ever met, she was like an exotic flower that you wanted to smell and touch and rub the soft petals across your cheek, but the second you did, there was nothing... you were dead if she wanted it to happen.

"Charlotte," Garret said my full name, and I loved hearing it on his lips. My whole body shivered, and my already sweaty palms slicked more. *Don't touch. Don't touch. Focus on the problem at hand, Charlie.*

I held up my hand to stop his advance. "Thank you for coming."

Garrett's eyes flashed with hurt at my denial, but it only lasted a second. Then anger burned brightly in his steely-blue eyes, along with a few flecks of yellow, but he pushed the magick away quickly.

Wetness pooled between my legs, and I sucked in a lungful of air. This wasn't going to be as easy as I'd thought.

"You called us to help you, Charlotte."

I stared at him and nodded, trying to push down the scorching desire to leap over the desk and rip his clothes from his body right there in front of everyone.

"Xerxes is trying to take control of the pack. My uncle wants this, and I can't let it happen. I need..." I blinked, trying to recall the words I'd rehearsed, but they wouldn't come back. All I had dancing in my head were visions of the three of us naked in my bed upstairs. I was losing my mind.

Time to try something else. "Rose. What brings you out of Sanctuary?" I didn't live in Sanctuary, but I'd visited enough to know that the matriarch of the town never left the Sisters of Lamidae—an ancient race of seers. The problems my pack were dealing with couldn't be reason enough to draw the queen of supernatural beings from the safety of her home.

Rose smiled. "We came to make sure that Travis and Garrett could assist you with your situation. It appears they are perfectly capable. Mikjáll and I will be traveling to Savannah with several others to rescue Riza's sister. Do you remember anything about another area where Xerxes may have spoken about keeping prisoners? Perhaps somewhere a governor lived?"

"He didn't. But I remember guards talking about transfers to and from a house. It may have been a governor's house now that you mention it." My brows crinkled, searching for the name, but I couldn't recall it. "Whitmarsh or march. I think they called it an island once."

Rose nodded. "Whitemarsh Island. Thank you, Charlie."

"Why does Xerxes have such an interest in Kitsune all of a sudden?"

The small woman shook her head. "It isn't sudden. We just didn't know about it. I should've seen it coming. The man is cunning, creative, and without morality."

"What is he doing?"

"Kitsune babies have a special property in their blood that allows another supernatural to merge it with their genetic makeup and use it to mask their non-human DNA."

"It turns us human?" I swallowed. It couldn't be. Why would Xerxes want to be human?

"No. It doesn't eliminate our supernatural DNA. It hides it from human blood tests or scans," she said, putting my initial fears to rest. "Kitsune are chameleons."

The last thing I wanted was to be human. I liked being a Lycan and couldn't imagine being anything but. But the ability to scientifically hide my species origin from tests was something any supernatural would want.

"Why do you want to stop him? Wouldn't we all benefit from a formula like that?"

Her eyes flashed white for a second, and her voice deepened. "I'm worried he'll kill the babies to harvest their blood, Charlie. Though I'm hoping he's smart enough to think long-term and not go to that extreme."

All thoughts of sex fled my mind, and my hormonally charged body lost control. Tears streamed down my cheeks. "Oh gods," I sobbed. "I didn't... Oh gods...I'm sure there are a couple of people who would go with you. Kate and Mallory both know the road to Savannah well. They could help you and show you the safe houses we have through the countryside."

Mikjáll stepped forward and shook his head. "We will not endanger anyone else from your pack, Charlie. We merely needed to know if you were aware of another place Xerxes used to hold prisoners. Travis and Garrett are here to help your pack heal."

I raised an eyebrow. The pack couldn't heal without an alpha pair taking control, and neither of the McLennon boys wanted to stay in Ada.

Unless something had changed.

I moved my focus from the Drakonae to Garrett's face. He'd moved closer to me while I'd been distracted by Rose and Mikjáll. Travis had come around the other side of the desk, approaching me from the left. Their earthy scent filled my lungs again, and my thumping heart kicked my ribs. The urge to throw myself into their arms surged inside me like a static charge. If I didn't touch them soon, I might spontaneously combust. Sweat beads ran from my forehead, trailing down my cheek and continuing down my neck until they came in contact with the t-shirt I was wearing.

"Thank you for coming to help me. I appreciate your support."

"Your parents were honorable people who always put others before themselves. Their daughter is the same. You know you and your pack have a home in Sanctuary, should you ever change your mind about staying here in Ada."

I shook my head. "Thank you. But this is my home, and I couldn't imagine ever leaving it or the people I love."

A smile spread across Rose's face. "Words of a true leader."

Heat from Travis' body warmed the air behind me. He wasn't touching me yet, but I knew he was only a hairsbreadth from doing so.

Don't touch me. Not yet.

I wanted him. I wanted them both as badly as I could see they wanted me. Their desire pulsed in each and every racing beat of their hearts, matching mine beat for beat. My breathing was shallow, and I struggled to maintain control over my trembling body.

When I called them to help, I didn't think the control I'd developed over my heat cycle would desert me so quickly, but I'd grossly underestimated my body's desire to join with my mates.

Rose inclined her head to me. "I'll let you three reacquaint yourselves. We need to be going. Travis," she said, "call Liam and a few others up from Sanctuary if anything happens with that emissary you can't handle on your own."

"I told him to leave," I said, standing straighter. But even as I argued, I knew she was right. He wasn't finished trying to convince the pack to turn against me.

"He'll be back, Charlie. All of you need to be prepared. Xerxes doesn't do anything halfway. There will be plans B, C, D, and more ideas beyond those."

"We will take good care of her and the pack, Rose," Garrett said, never once dropping his gaze from me.

CHAPTER
SEVEN

XERXES

The clicking of high heels approached from across the massive room I used as my office in the Whitemarsh Mansion outside of Savannah, the new capital of the South East Coast Republic.

"What's the status?" I asked without looking up from my desk. Running a damn country without *it* knowing I was running it was beginning to try my nerves. I closed the file on my desk, slamming my hand down hard on the thick stack of problems. Everything would be much simpler once I eliminated the human puppet who acted as the SECR's president-elect.

But first I needed a viable sample of the Kitsune infant's blood to bond with mine. Since losing Riza and the child she'd been carrying, her sister was my only source, and I'd damn anyone to the pits of Hades, even Manda, if they tried to take her from me.

Kitsune babies were the key to everything now.

Sochi delivered her first baby months ago and was already pregnant with a second. Since the second pregnancy started, I'd eliminated all her outings and put her on drug-induced bed-rest, but not before making sure she made an appearance on the news. If Riza saw her sister, she would come back and perhaps I could bring her back into my breeding program.

Djinn guards and loyal Lycans I'd brought over to my side patrolled the mansion. Lycans who hated humans and wanted to see them pay for the atrocities they'd brought down on their species. Finding those who had a thirst for vengeance hadn't been hard.

Supernaturals either wanted peace or wanted to rule. Manipulating people who were greedy for power and revenge was easy.

I glanced up at Manda's shapely body. She wore a tailored black business suit and a sheer blouse beneath the jacket. She always attempted to hide her figure, but I knew exactly what she tried to hide. Normally I would ask her to strip and bend over my desk before delivering her report. But today was different. Today, she was bringing me the report from the lab.

"Well?" I asked, impatient to see what was in the blue file folder in her hand. "Give it to me."

She laid the file on the desk quickly and backed away.

A grin tugged at my mouth, and I lifted one hand, grabbing her around the neck with my magick. She choked as I pulled her closer. Her shoes scraped against the floor as she fought the invisible leash.

"Why do you try? You are at my mercy. You will

always be at my mercy. Even that Phoenix didn't have the heart to put you out of your misery."

Her bright eyes, sapphire blue from the contacts she wore to hide their natural lavender color, widened. The lustrous olive tint of her skin was beginning to pale as I starved her of oxygen.

A moment later, her eyes closed and she stopped struggling. I tossed her across the room and picked up the file she'd delivered –the lab report on the latest trial. Skimming it quickly, I passed over all the boring data until my eyes alighted on the single red word at the bottom of the page.

POSITIVE

I read on, burying the urge to shout in celebration. Finally.

Subject showed no signs of illness in the first twenty-four hours. Subject is now testing POSITIVE for human on all blood-related tests.

I flipped the page. Where was the trial on the scanning equipment we'd stolen from the Washington Republic? Why didn't I have data on that?

Glaring across the room at Manda's unconscious body, I growled.

The lack of data from the second trial was no doubt why she'd been so fidgety. So much for getting through the meeting without fucking her a couple of times. I suddenly needed to release some frustration, and she was going to oblige me. My earlier generosity had vanished when I realized the trials with the Kitsune blood were once again running behind schedule.

The idiots in the lab had assured me weeks ago that

they were almost finished, yet each test had come back with negative side effects or inconclusive data. Screw the data.

Apparently, Manda wasn't motivating them enough. I was quite sick of waiting. She was going soft on me. As much as I tortured her, she continued to thwart my progress. These delays were either a passive aggressive way of fighting me or a desperate attempt to try and force me to kill her once and for all.

No chance.

Standing from my desk, I turned and tugged on the painting that hung on the wall. It swung out silently, revealing the wall safe I'd had installed behind it. After punching in the code, I opened the thick steel door and plucked one of the *quppa* boxes from the bottom shelf. These boxes held Manda's specific motivation. Over the centuries, I'd only had to kill off three people.

This would be the fourth. I wondered which person from her old life—the life where she'd been a queen of her people—was locked in this particular box. Would it be family? An old lover? I hadn't opened the one with her mother yet. That would make for an interesting afternoon and certainly distract me from the disappointment of yet another failure.

Manda stirred on the floor, and I heard the telltale intake of breath that signaled she'd once again regained consciousness.

"You brought this on yourself. You haven't done your job to the best of your ability, and you know there are always consequences for failing your assignments."

She snarled, showing a little of the fight she used to

have. The smug arrogance that led to her downfall and enslavement to me. To the enslavement of her entire kingdom and race.

"Ah, ah, ah," I said, moving my pointer finger back and forth like a parent would warn a child. Then I pointed downward to the *quppa* box sitting on my desk.

She dove into a prostrate position on her knees, her hands stretched wide and her forehead plastered against the rug that decorated the center of the room.

"Please," she begged, her voice trembling and barely louder than a whisper. "I'll do whatever you want."

"You were supposed to deliver two reports to me today. And now there will be a consequence for failure."

"They weren't done. The equipment malfunctioned. It was reading everyone incorrectly. They are working on it, I swear!" she said. The tone of her voice rose with each word. She wasn't trying to hide her desperation.

"I warned you that each failure would result in the death of one of your people."

"Please, just hurt me. Do what you will to me. They don't deserve this!" She rose from her position on the floor and launched herself at the desk.

Her desperate attempt didn't surprise me. I caught her with my magick mid-leap.

"Arthur! Weston! Get in here," I bellowed. It was about time those two Lycan guards witnessed my wrath. Word would spread among their ranks and worked better than a threat directed at them.

Two large Lycan men bustled into the room.

"Hold her," I said, pointing to Manda as she appeared to be floating in mid-air.

"Sir?"

I waved my hand, releasing her from my magick, and her body dropped to the ground with a pleasant *thud*. "Hold her."

They both nodded and rushed forward, each grabbing her by an arm and pulling her into an upright position.

"You fucking bastard!" she screamed at me, her eyes glowing brightly, showing lavender through the contacts. "Stop! Xerxes, stop!" Her struggle was futile. The two Lycan's were both a foot taller and a hundred pounds heavier.

She was nothing without her powers. And lately, her keen mind was more of a nuisance than a benefit to my long-term plans. Still, I'd worked many years to get her into the high-ranking position of Director of Defense in the SECR human government. Manda's very existence allowed me to control the entire SECR military without anyone being the wiser.

I picked up the little black box and whispered the ancient phrase that would release its prisoner.

"Run! Run! Run!" she screamed, over and over.

"Cover her mouth!" I bellowed.

They complied, and her warnings became nothing more than muffled moans, but it didn't stop her from kicking and writhing in their grasp. I would enjoy fucking the fight out of her after this. She was always more enjoyable when she was riled and angry.

Risk was to be expected when releasing a being who was probably thousands of years old. They didn't live that long because they were stupid. I had only a nanosecond to catch the prisoner between the time they materialized and the time they realized they needed to blink away from the situation.

A person materialized a few feet to my left.

It was a woman. *Good. I especially like killing women.* She cocked her head to the side, staring at me in confusion. A string of ancient Persian fell from her lips, and then she noticed Manda struggling to her left across the room. But by then it was too late.

I squeezed my fist in the air and smiled as my magick tightened around the woman's neck.

A second later, another Djinn blinked into the room. "Sir, guards in the..." His voice cut off when his gaze fell on the woman I was choking. "No!"

I used my other hand to reach for him, but he blinked away before I got a grasp on his essence. "Fucking Djinn always have the worst timing and no manners." Who was the mystery woman? Apparently, the messenger had recognized her and was willing to cross me personally.

Pain shot through my back, and I gasped for breath. My magick faltered just long enough, and the other woman was gone before I could regain control. He stabbed me again and again, and I whirled, magick flowing like molten lava from my body. I fisted my hands together and then pulled them apart, using my magick to viciously separate his head from his body.

I turned from the gruesome scene to the guards where they held a now-sobbing Manda. My clothes were ruined from the stab wounds, but they were healing quickly. In a few hours, there wouldn't even be a scar.

He hadn't been trying to kill me, but I would've liked to know where he got his hands on a dragon-steel blade.

Picking it up from the floor where he dropped it, I twirled the blade in my hand. Only dragon steel could cut me. And only a dragon-steel blade forged in dragon-fire could truly hurt or kill me. Blades forged in the fire of a Drakonae's breath left a thin coating of poison deadly only to Lamassu. This one was not the latter or I'd already be feeling the effects of the dragon-fire poison.

No. This had merely been a distraction. A sacrifice to enable the mystery woman to escape her fate. He'd died to give her a chance to escape.

I'd find her again, sooner than later. An ancient Persian Djinn who didn't speak any other languages wouldn't be too hard to track.

It was yet another hiccup in my day, and Manda would be punished for it.

"Strip her."

CHAPTER EIGHT

TRAVIS

She smelled so good. Sweet. Ready to mate. The sweat shining on her skin was filled with hormones that signaled her desire. A glance at my brother acknowledged that we both felt the same pull.

At first, it'd caused strife between us that Charlie had called to both our magick. Trios between Lycans weren't unheard of, but it was rare enough to make both of us pause. We'd shared women before, but never considered Fate actually matching us in a triad.

Neither of us spoke again until the screen door slammed closed after Mikjáll and Rose exited the lodge.

Charlie whirled and backed away from me, putting herself closer to Garrett in the process. He stepped forward, and she came toward me again, trapped and wide-eyed, but panting for the same thing we all equally needed.

Release from the mating heat.

"Why are you fighting it?" I growled, advancing close.

She took a deep breath and straightened her back. Her strength and independence would make her an amazing alpha female. Unfortunately, that was probably what held her back from accepting us. The pack was everything to her, and she wouldn't abandon them to come back with us to Sanctuary.

Garrett and I had discussed it, though, and if Charlie gave us the chance, we would stay with her and make the Ada pack our home. We'd already brought up the possibility with Rose, and she'd given her blessing. Not that we needed it, but when you lived under the protection of the most powerful being on earth, being polite was a given.

"I have to do what the pack needs. I can't be with either of you if the pack isn't your first priority." There it was. She didn't beat around the bush. "This pack has always been about helping other Lycans. Not just protecting our family, but protecting all."

"Charlotte. We've done anything and everything Rose ever asked of us to protect the inhabitants of Sanctuary—Lycan or not. What makes you think we wouldn't accept the bond to your pack if we mated?" Garrett advanced another step closer to her trembling form.

She sucked in a deep breath and shook from head to foot. "This is a lifetime commitment. I don't want to move to Sanctuary, not unless the entire pack votes and chooses that path."

A growled vibrated deep in my chest. "We came to make a commitment to you, Charlie. That means we are committing to your pack, too. We understand the responsibility that comes with being alpha. I would've been alpha in my old pack. I'm no stranger to making the right choice for the whole, instead of myself."

"I feel the same, Charlotte," Garrett said, lifting a hand to her shoulder.

She didn't flinch, and I took a step forward as well, until she was within arm's reach. Leaning down, I nuzzled her ear.

"We need you as much as you need us, Charlie," I whispered.

"We are here for you and your pack. They will be our pack," Garrett said, moving his head to the other side of her face. "But first we must satisfy the bond."

She rubbed her cheek against mine and then his before a slow sigh slipped between her lips. Her body shuddered, and I placed a hand on the rise of her breast, reveling in the racing beat of her heart against her ribs.

"Where's your room?" I asked.

The energy building within her body was nearly ready to burst. She'd been able to control her heat cycle with us a few hours away, but now... Her wolf would have what it wanted.

Us.

"Upstairs," she breathed. "The blue door at the end of the hallway." Her arms encircled my neck, and she squeezed tight, lifting her lower body and wrapping her legs around my waist.

Garrett growled excitedly behind her, and I caught his hungry gaze over her shoulder. He nearly took the office door off the hinges as he yanked it open. I followed directly behind him, carrying her easily across the mostly empty living area. I caught some quizzical looks from a few pack females, but no one questioned that we were obviously taking their alpha female upstairs to claim.

My feet pounded on the stairs after Garrett's. A few moments later, we were standing in her bedroom, taking in the gravity of what we were about to do. She was right. Taking on the mantle of alpha for a devastated pack wouldn't be a picnic, but he and I had seen our fair share of horrible. Whether she knew it or not, we could and would support her and the pack through this transition.

I could only hope that assisting her pack would also help heal the wounds I buried in my heart from failing my family—my whole pack. Garrett's wounds ran deep, but he hadn't been preparing to be an alpha back then. Still, the pain had been so profound that neither of us could stay together. We'd separated for decades, only just recently reuniting in Sanctuary this past year.

Now we'd found our Fated mate. Both of us. Together.

"Stop thinking, Travis, and start stripping," Charlie said, sliding from my grasp. She tugged at the hem of my shirt a moment later. "You, too, Garrett," she said, glancing over her shoulder. "I need you both so badly my body will literally come apart at the seams if I can't have you *right* now."

"I'd hate to keep my mate waiting," Garrett answered, a grin splitting his face in half.

The hard dick in my pants agreed with both of them.

After chucking my shirt across the room, Charlie grabbed the bottom of hers and pulled it over her head, revealing a black lacy bra and the most perfectly rounded breasts I could've imagined. I wanted to taste them, and she could tell. Her eyes glinted with excitement and desire. My hands moved even faster, divesting my body of any scrap of clothing I'd been wearing.

She shimmied out of her jeans and panties. Garrett's hands made short work of the hook on her bra while she stepped out of everything. The bra fell to the floor, freeing her breasts from their lacy confines.

A slight gasp slipped from between her lips as she stood, baring herself proudly to the both of us. We approached, one on each side. She turned to Garrett this time, caressing his face as I ran a palm down the side of her hip and over the round globe of her ass.

Slipping my fingers between her legs, I pressed through her folds, pleased to find her slick and wet and needy.

"Hmmmm," she moaned, arching her backside against my raging hard-on. It took every ounce of willpower not to bend her over the bed and take her in that moment. But she wasn't just mine.

Garrett and I had shared women before, but Charlie was different. She wasn't just a fuck. She was our mate. We would love and treasure her above everything else in our lives.

She was ours. Only ours.

"Is she ready for us, brother?" Garrett asked, his eyes hooded and flashing gold.

I raised my eyebrows and smiled. "Abso-fucking-lutely."

CHAPTER NINE

CHARLIE

Energy coursed through me with each caress and nuzzle and breath that touched my overheated, magickally charged body. My lady bits dripped with my arousal, and my heart raced in my chest, threatening to leap free from the confines of my rib cage at any moment.

I needed them. Desperately.

Amidst everything, guilt coursed through my mind. I was about to have sex with two of the sexiest Lycan men I'd ever met. The first hint of their crisp, spicy scent in the lodge had sent my body careening back into a full-blown heat.

Xerxes had Lycans in Ada trying to convince the pack to surrender, instigating disloyalty from my uncle and cousin and probably others. And here I was, focused solely on getting 'busy' with the two men who were supposed to be my mates.

I tried to convince myself that this was what needed to happen first. That all three of us would be worthless to the pack until we sated and sealed the bond burning between the three of us.

Fate did not like to be denied. And I wasn't about to fight her any longer. Staying away from Travis and Garrett had been torture. But asking them to take my pack on--our problems, our wounds--as their own was a lot.

They said they were up for it, but I still wondered how committed they would be over the long haul... or if we would immediately go back to fighting about moving to Sanctuary.

They'd made a home in the mixed up menagerie that was Sanctuary. Pixies, Vampires, Lycans, Drakonae, and other species all called the small town their home. But I grew up in Ada, and I didn't want to leave. I didn't want to ask my family to pick up and move. In Sanctuary, we wouldn't be a pack of our own. We'd be assimilated into the democratic mix of packs that lived there.

We would lose our autonomy. Our mission.

I couldn't do that to my parents. In honor of their life-long struggle, we had to stay and fight, to support those who couldn't support themselves.

"Where are you, Charlotte?" Garrett asked, running his thumb over one of my erect nipples. I shivered at the stimulation and arched my chest into his hand, encouraging his fondling.

Travis' warm body pressed against me from behind while Garrett leaned closer from the front. Both men had hard-ons that made every muscle in my body tense with anticipation. I'd never been with two men at once before, but they seemed perfectly comfortable with sharing, which allowed any shadow of apprehension to fade away.

These were two powerful Lycans who were fated to both be my mates. After this, they would be connected to me forever. We would bond and seal our souls.

Their hands guided me to the bed.

Garrett climbed in first and sat against the headboard. He motioned for me to face away from him, and I turned to face Travis as I sat between Garrett's legs and reclined against his sinewy chest.

My head was close enough to his that he could lean down and kiss me at his pleasure. He slid his hands beneath my arms and reached around, cupping each of my breasts, tugging me tight against him as Travis crawled up onto my bed.

I caught Travis' gaze and licked my lips, letting myself glance down his perfectly sculpted body to the large cock jutting from a bed of dark blonde curls.

Travis ran his hands up my legs, catching hold just below each knee and pushing gently until my legs were drawn up and my thighs were very close to brushing against my torso.

He scooted closer, leaning down for a kiss. His mouth captured mine, and he nipped my bottom lip with his teeth.

A moan slipped out, and I pushed against his grip, trying to straighten my legs and body from the pretzel they had folded me into. I gripped Garrett's biceps as he rolled my pebbled nipples between his fingers.

Travis' cock nudged at my opening, and seconds later,

he'd filled me completely. I gasped from the fullness. The warmth of his body pressed me harder into Garrett's chest. He pumped slowly and deeply, and the magick inside me swirled at the top. My canines tried to descend, but it wasn't time.

I panted through breath after breath.

He sped up his thrusts, and Garrett murmured words of praise into my ear. How beautiful I was. How much he couldn't wait to feel my pussy around his hard cock. How they were going to make me call out both their names when they took me together and sealed our mate bond.

"Yes," I moaned out. I wanted it. Every cell of my body craved it. They were the other half of me. The part I'd desired for so long. A mate. A family. Babies.

Something more than the fight against humans or the silent war with Xerxes.

The pleasure built and built, but he never let me get close enough to climax. Sweat slicked all three of us by the time Travis pulled away and motioned for his brother to switch places with him.

I snarled. "Wait, I…" Travis covered my mouth with his and plunged his tongue deep, tasting every facet of my mouth. Garrett was between my legs in a moment, hooking them over his shoulders and driving the hard erection I'd been leaning against between my slick folds.

Air whooshed from my lungs, and I gulped, fighting for the breath they were both determined to steal from me. I needed to come, and they somehow knew exactly when my body started to crest, because both of them would back off.

"It's gonna be worth it, sweetheart," Garrett growled

as he slid deep inside. My toes curled, and my thighs contracted on his shoulders, drawing him closer.

Travis loosed my lips, and I stretched my head forward. Garrett rewarded my effort with a tender kiss, sweeping his tongue through my mouth, before sucking first my top lip between his teeth and then my bottom lip.

"Please," I begged between each thrust of his pelvis.

"Not until we are as one, Charlie," Travis whispered into my ear from behind me.

"Now, now, now," I panted, as an orgasm began coiling deep in my abdomen. "I need it now." My fangs descended and a growl rumbled in my chest.

"I think she's ready, brother," Travis said, humor coloring his voice.

Garrett caught my gaze and nodded. He pulled out and backed up a little. Travis' hands closed around my waist and lifted, sliding down from the headboard until I was straddling him. He brought me down straight onto his erection.

"Ahhhhh," I gasped again.

Garrett smiled and climbed off the bed. "Travis is going to take your pussy, sweetheart, and I'm going to fill that sweet ass of yours, but first I need to play with it."

I nodded, watching him over my shoulder as Travis lifted and pulled me down over, again and again, distracting me from what Garrett said he was going to do. I knew how the triad bond would seal. I just hadn't considered the actual act yet.

"Put that ass in the air for Garrett, baby" Travis ordered, lifting me off of his glorious cock again, leaving me empty and wanting.

The drawer of my nightstand slid shut with a thud. "You've got a nice collection here, love." Garrett's voice deepened, and another shiver ran across my skin.

He knelt on the bed behind me, and my only warning before cold lube fell between my ass cheeks was the snap of a bottle lid. I tensed at first as Garrett worked the gel into the tight rosebud of muscles.

The pressure was unfamiliar, but arousing.

"Don't come yet, love. That's an order."

An order? The way his finger slipped in and out had my legs quivering. I clung to Travis' waist, pressing my face into his chest, moaning each time Garrett's finger entered me. I wanted to come. *Now.*

"You are so beautiful, Charlotte. So fucking beautiful."

Travis pushed me to my hands, giving himself full access to my breasts. He tweaked my nipples and smiled. "Do you like having Garrett's finger in your ass, Charlie?"

"Mmmmhmmm." Coherent words and thoughts had fled my consciousness. I wanted. No. Needed one thing.

To come.

The lid of a bottle snapped again, and the cold sensation of the fresh gel mixed with Garrett added another finger to my virgin hole.

So tight. Gods, it burned and made my body sing at the same time. The pain melted into more pleasure, and I rocked backward against his hand, taking more. As he scissored his fingers inside my ass, slowly stretching and pulling the muscles open a little at a time, his other hand fondled my pussy. He rubbed a finger around my throbbing clit, but was careful never to directly touch it, somehow sensing that one slip would send me careening into bliss.

"Please." I let my head drop backward gently and whimpered. My sex throbbed with a need so overwhelming all I could think about was the crest of my impending climax.

"How's she doing up there?"

"So tight. I can't wait to put my cock deep inside her ass. Do you hear that, Charlotte?"

"Mmmmmm," I moaned again, feeling more delicious burn as he added a third finger. "I need you. Both of you."

"We have to go slow, sweetheart." Garrett fondled my clit and pushed his fingers a little deeper. I gulped for breath as my entire body tensed under the pressure.

"Relax into it, Charlie." Travis' voice lulled me loose from the tension and the uncomfortable tightness faded into decadent pleasure.

Garrett began moving his fingers in and out until there wasn't much resistance left.

"You ready to try this, sweetheart?"

"Yes, please."

"How much do you need to come?" Travis asked, his deep voice lusty and teasing.

"Please. Yes." My words didn't answer his question, but coherent thought had long since fled my mind.

Travis re-situated us on the bed so that he was buried inside me while leaving my ass open and ready for Garrett.

I wiggled on his cock, shaking my bottom.

"Impatient little wolf," Garrett said, another chuckle rolling up from his chest.

"She is." Travis reached up and grabbed the back of my head, pulling me down for a delicious kiss.

Garrett moved into place behind me and began working at the tight rosebud with the head of his cock. Pushing and pulling just the head, in and out, giving me time to adjust to the penetration. His fingers had done an excellent job of prepping me and the stretch from his cock felt wickedly good.

Travis' mouth on my nipples distracted me somewhat from being filled with two cocks.

"That's it, sweetheart." Pain sent a shudder through my body, and I fought to continue to breathe as I took more of Garrett's cock.

Travis remained still while Garrett worked patiently and slowly, giving my body time to stretch. The pain slowly turned from a burn to a feeling of completeness that I hadn't dreamed was possible.

A contented groan slipped from Garrett's mouth. Once he'd seated himself completely, he moved in and out a few times before they started taking turns. Their alternating thrusts were almost too much.

The orgasm coiling inside me swirled to life and roared forward, shaking me to my core. My body contracted around them both, and a scream tore from my throat as I came.

Magick warmed my skin, and my canines descended again. I buried them in Travis' shoulder, marking him as my permanent mate. A male roar followed my bite, and

Travis bit down into my shoulder, giving me the same mate mark, as his seed filled my womb.

A second later, Garrett followed with his climax. He waited until Travis and I released each other before lifting me off of his brother. My legs were useless, and his strong arms supported me as he turned me to face him.

His eyes were bright yellow. Desire burned, and I bared my neck, offering him the unbitten side to mark. I would wear two mate marks, and at this very moment, I couldn't have been more pleased. My wolf certainly was.

Garrett bit, and pain surged from the bite, but morphed into an endorphin high that amped up my wolf again. I dug my fingers into his upper arms, pulling myself higher in his grasp. He released my neck, and I growled as I buried my fangs in his, giving him a bite to match the one I'd given his brother.

Peace settled over me. The fire that had burned from inside out cooled as the magick that connected the three of us now fell into place around me, a blanket of security. Our scents mingled and would forever be mixed as long as the three of us lived. We would always be able to find the others, no matter where we were or how far we were from each other.

I nuzzled Garrett's chest and sighed. His arms tightened around me, and he kissed the top of my head.

"Let's wash up, sweetheart, and then cuddle up in this little bed of yours," he said.

Nodding my head slowly, I murmured my agreement.

"Travis?" He spoke to his brother over my shoulder.

"On it." The springs on my bed squeaked as the huge

Lycan jumped up. He disappeared into the bathroom off my bedroom, and soon, water was running in the shower.

Garrett scooped me into his arms and carried my well-used, limp body to the shower. Both men attended to me, scrubbing and kissing and washing every inch of my skin until I was shaking all over again from desire.

Denied round two, I settled for being tucked between them on my bed after we finished in the shower.

CHAPTER
TEN

GARRETT

The dark cloud of unease that had followed me since first realizing Charlotte was our mate had disappeared the second I kissed her this evening. Our scents were mixed, and I could not only smell myself on her skin, I could smell Travis, too. She was our treasure. In a way, she'd probably brought us closer than we would've ever gotten on our own if we had married or mated separately.

I stared at the beam ceiling. Moonlight softly illuminated the room through one window draped with a sheer white curtain.

Fate seemed to have done all of us a favor with this match. We all equally needed the others to survive what the world had thrown our way. We were all orphans and shared the pain of watching our parents' lives being taken right in front of us.

At that time, nothing worse could've happened. I

think I blamed Travis as much as he blamed me. We'd drifted apart after losing them until something... unexplainable happened last year.

I heard about Sanctuary through an underground Lycan group and couldn't put it out of my mind. I hadn't seen my brother in decades, and for some reason, I felt the need to check this one little small town on the off-chance that he was there.

A shot in a million. But it'd proven worthwhile. Not only had my brother taken up residence in the tiny West Texas town, he was in deep with the people who ran Sanctuary, a refuge for supernatural beings.

Sanctuary, Texas was more than just a safe harbor, but everyone was pretty quiet about the reasons behind a lot of activities that occurred within the city limits. The woman who ran the place was a being who shouldn't even exist anymore. Lamassu had been extinct for thousands of years... or so everyone in the supernatural community had been led to believe. Of course, we didn't know any Drakonae had made it through the Veil, either. Supernatural history was mostly passed down orally, and a lot had been lost over the millennia. Plus, most species tended to only teach their children about *their* history. My parents had only passed along history and legends that belonged to the Lycan race.

According to the stories I'd heard, the Lycans had been one of the very first species to explore the Earth side of the portal gate.

A light footfall on the eve of the rooftop outside Charlotte's bedroom window raised my hackles. Travis snored lightly on the opposite side of the bed, spooning Charlotte with a hand tucked possessively over her hip.

I raised my head and studied the night sky through the half-covered window. The footfall was strange. No one was awake in the lodge. No one had moved around the lodge in several hours. I certainly would've heard if someone had exited the building. The doors weren't exactly quiet.

A second later, I squinted when a red light passed through my gaze. Then a red dot flickered on my bare chest.

Fuck. The thought crossed my mind just as pain exploded inside my chest, and the sound of a shattering window brought me to high alert. I gasped for air and roared, anger driving my beast quickly from its relaxed state to yanking at the leash begging to spill blood.

Charlotte sat up between us and shrieked.

Several more shots echoed through the otherwise quiet night, and Travis leapt from the bed to the window, grabbing the muzzle of the gun pointed into the bedroom and wrenching it from the man holding it.

I coughed, tasting the metallic flavor of blood.

I rolled to cover our mate's body, but the pain spreading in my chest made me collapse on top of her. At least a bullet would have to go all the way through me before it found an inch of her flesh.

"Garrett," she whimpered, pushing against my blood-slicked chest. "Travis, he's been shot!"

A couple more shots went off before I heard my brother's voice through the roar of my pounding pulse.

"Are they dead?" Charlotte asked quietly, pushing against my chest as Travis helped me crawl off of her.

"Two are, but one got away. I couldn't risk leaving the two of you longer. There could have been another attack coming from inside the house."

I tried to speak again, but only succeeded in coughing up more blood.

"Don't try to talk, Garrett." He grabbed a corner of the sheet and stuffed it into my mouth then retrieved his k-bar from his jeans pocket. "This is gonna hurt like a bitch."

Fuck.

The pain from him digging out the bullet brought me very close to passing out.

"Give the magick a few minutes to start to mend that." Travis felt along my bare shoulder and then along my shoulder blade. "It was just one shot?"

I nodded, slowly spitting the wadded up sheet corner from my mouth.

The attackers were Lycan. Their scent permeated the room through the open window, and it made me want to tear something apart.

"The house is awake," Travis said, his voice deep and solemn. Frantic shouts and heavy footfalls sounded downstairs and upstairs as the entire lodge roused to find out what had disturbed their home.

"Charlie!" a female voice called from the hallway.

"We're good," Travis hollered. "Is anyone else hurt?"

The door flew open, and a blonde female Lycan stepped into the dimly lit bedroom. "Who got hurt?"

"My brother. Can you send people out to check the

perimeter and bring me a few clean towels?"

She nodded. "Victor is already leading a group out to follow the men who dared to attack our home."

"Was any other part of the lodge breached, Kara?" Charlotte asked.

The female shook her head. "All the noise came from your room. We can't find a breach anywhere else," she said before ducking into the en suite bathroom.

"They were Lycans," I growled, finally able to speak. The magick worked quickly. In minutes, the wound had sealed. In a day's time, there wouldn't even be a scar from the encounter.

A male appeared in the hall doorway wearing an expression that would've frightened even the most stalwart of humans. "Why would Lycans attack our lodge?" His eyes glowed bright gold, and his canines were descended and bared.

"Because Charlotte opposed them," I bit out. "What did you think Xerxes would do when you told him 'no'? He's not exactly flexible. He wants control by any means necessary."

The female spoke again, returning from the bathroom with two large towels. She handed them to Travis and Charlotte. "But when they left this afternoon, Victor told them the pack would vote on the decision and get him an answer tomorrow. Why attack before we have a chance to get back to them? I don't understand. Who does that help?"

It helps Victor. With the two of us and Charlotte dead, he would be able to take control of the pack without a fight.

CHAPTER
ELEVEN

CHARLIE

A snarl fell from my lips. "He spoke to the emissary again after I dismissed him?"

Kara nodded. "He's supposed to come back around noon. This is crazy, Charlie. We can't live this way."

"Kara, you can't possibly believe the story he told. Xerxes doesn't offer peace treaties. It's a trick. Victor is playing right into their hands. Except he's going to hand all of you over on a silver platter without even realizing it." I glanced down at the towel I'd pressed to Garrett's chest. It was dry beneath my hand, and I took a deep breath, satisfied that my mate was going to be fine. The wound had already closed.

"Victor has a point, Charlie. This pack has seen enough tragedy. Maybe it's time to stop fighting. I know that's not what you want to hear, but how do I support you when the choices you and your parents made cost me my brother and my mate?"

"We fight for those who can't help themselves, Kara. Your brother and your mate understood that and wanted to help. I never forced anyone to volunteer." She'd lost friends, family, her parents. Kara wasn't the only one who'd lost someone important. "I watched my parents die. My friends. Fighting for this pack is something I will never stop doing."

"If you can't see that Victor probably arranged this attack as an assassination attempt on your alphas, you don't deserve to stay a part of this pack," Travis snarled, standing from the edge of the bed.

The male behind Kara, Crawley, stepped forward to protect her from Travis' implied threat. "Watch your step, outsider. Just because you've fucked the Mason heir doesn't mean you get to threaten us."

Moving faster than I imagined possible. I spun, swinging my foot out, knocking Crawley to the ground. My fingers wrapped around his throat, and I pinned the larger man to the floor, putting my fingers directly over his carotid artery.

Travis was no more than a foot behind me, ready to tear the disrespectful Lycan to bits if he so much as twitched wrong.

"If you speak to my mate again in such a tone, I will let him treat it as a challenge, and you will suffer the consequences." My tone stayed level and controlled, but Crawley's eyes widened as they focused on Travis' huge form looming above us both. "This pack has been through hell, but we aren't going to get to a better place if we turn on each other. Help us, Crawley. Don't fight us."

Crawley nodded, and I slowly released the fatal grip I had on his neck. Standing swiftly, I moved toward Travis and patted him on the arm before disappearing into my bedroom again to check on Garrett.

My other mate was well on his way to being mended. He was sitting on the edge of the bed, wiping his chest of smeared blood. The wound had completely closed, and he was as agitated as Travis, no doubt from hearing the rash words that had fallen out of Crawley's mouth.

"This situation *is* going to take a formal challenge, Charlotte," Garrett said, taking my hand and pulling me to sit next to him on the edge of the bed.

"I don't want more fighting," I answered, shaking my head. A formal challenge meant another death, and I wasn't about to gamble with the life of either of my mates.

"You may not have a choice," he said, his voice rumbling with an authority I'd only ever heard from Travis. "This is our pack, too. We are responsible for your safety and the safety of every man, woman, and child inside these walls."

"Garrett is right." Travis approached the bed and sat on my other side. "When a pack goes through as much as this one, sometimes the only way to create order again is to force it."

"No," I growled. "I won't let you. Victor may have it out for me, but he'd never knowingly put the rest of the pack in danger. When he gets back, we will talk. I can make him understand."

"You can try, sweetheart," Garrett said, wrapping an arm around my shoulder. "But if you won't let us do what we feel is necessary, the only other option is leaving."

No. This couldn't be happening. They thought they could take me away from my pack. Mate or not, I would never leave, and they couldn't force me if they ever wanted the privilege of sleeping with me again.

The door opened and slammed shut a few times, and I glanced at Travis and Garrett. They nodded to the dresser, and I frowned. I grabbed one of the clean towels Kara had put on the bed and wiped Garrett's blood from my skin. Then hurried to my dresser and pulled on a pair of yoga shorts, a sports bra, and a tank top before dashing through the open bedroom door.

Nudity wasn't a huge thing in the lodge. We all shifted in front of each other for runs, but being dressed for a confrontation with my uncle and cousin, who were trying to usurp my authority, was certainly better than trying to do it in the buff.

Travis and Garrett struggled to pull on their jeans before pounding down the hall after me. When I paused in the living room, Garrett stopped next to me, still buttoning his pants.

Victor sat in my father's captain chair, and the fucking emissary from Xerxes sat in my mother's. Rational thought fled my mind at that point, and I lunged with a roar, surprised to find my body suspended in mid-air by Garrett's strong arms.

"I'll kill him! Put me down! The nerve."

My uncle caught my gaze, and there was nothing. No guilt. No remorse. No emotion that I could see of any kind. If he and Dean were playing me or had allowed the hit on my bedroom, they were playing it close to the vest.

The emissary twitched in his chair, a little more uncomfortable with my rage than my uncle.

I opened my mouth to scream again, but Travis stepped in front of me, picking up the alpha mantle as though he'd always worn it.

"You are not welcome in this den. The attempt on my brother and my mate will not go unpunished. If those Lycan soldiers were yours, prepare to lose them. They will not return home with you." His voice thundered though the living area, and the other pack members shrank against the walls as the intensity of his alpha power started to spread through the room. My rage took an instant back seat, my wolf immediately willing to bow to his wishes.

Dammit. He better not use this against me.

Garrett released me, probably realizing I wasn't a danger to anyone's throat any longer. As my mate, he was alpha as well, but like me, our wolves' nature would naturally defer to Travis. He was the oldest male in our triad. The prime alpha.

Magick rolled from Travis in waves, and my uncle shifted nervously in his chair.

"I had nothing to do with the attack on you or your mate," the emissary growled, standing.

Brave words for a man with two angry alpha Lycans only a few feet away. I was used to taking care of myself, but having them there, standing up for me... for the pack. This was a good thing.

Travis' head cocked to the side, and he took a step

closer to the heavy-breathing, traitorous-smelling Lycan visitor. He leaned in close and sniffed.

"I smell fear, which means somewhere there's a lie. If you're still in *my* den by the time I count to five, I'll beat you into the gravel parking lot outside until all that's left are bits and pieces for the ravens to feast on. We'll see if your men come back after witnessing that." His icy voice sent a chill down my spine, and the threat wasn't directed at me.

The emissary fled the room, leaving the front door wide open as he excused himself from the lodge.

Travis' gaze fell to Dean, who stood not quite so proudly as before behind Victor's chair. But Victor hadn't moved and didn't appear to be considering giving even an inch of recognition to his new alphas.

"This is not your den or your pack. She is not worthy of the name she bears." Victor's voice was calculating and cold. "She's brought only death and sorrow to our pack, just like her father and mother. But no more," he continued, standing from his chair.

My body temperature rocketed straight to boiling. How dare he just try and sweep me to the side! I took a step forward, but Garrett caught my arm.

"This fight is for us to win in your stead. It is not the place of the alpha female to fight for her position," he whispered, drawing my body flush to his.

"The emissary is lying to you, Victor. Sanctuary has dealt with Xerxes many years longer than you have. He is a liar and related to the devil himself. This deal brought before you is bogus. Death will be your only reward for agreeing to his 'idea' of peace. He will slaughter you like the fool you are." Travis glanced over to Dean and the large group of Lycans standing along the wall behind him. "And you all, as well. Along with what few loved ones and children you have left."

"We don't have the ability to fight anyone," growled a female from the back of the room. "If we don't take a chance with the treaty, he'll kill us all anyway."

"Shut up, Lisa!" Victor snarled.

Travis shook his head. "We will fight for you. Sanctuary will fight for all of you."

A growl rumbled in my chest. "We don't belong to Sanctuary."

"Sanctuary will still fight for you. Whether you stay here in Ada or choose to move," Travis answered, swinging his head to the left to catch my gaze.

I nodded, breathing a sigh of relief. Travis and Garrett were respecting my choice, but each time something came up, fear surged forward revealing that they didn't really intend to make this their permanent home.

Trusting them was something I would have to get used to.

"You're an outsider," a male called out from the back of the room. "We're better off staying loyal to family. We don't know you or your brother. Victor is pack and family by blood."

"Victor is going to get you killed, William. Not once did my father ever say the alpha line should go to Victor. I have my Fated matches standing with me. Our laws are satisfied. This discussion is tantamount to mutiny." I took a step forward, moving to stand next to Travis. Garrett moved to stand at my other shoulder.

Both men dwarfed me, but neither spoke to counter what I'd said.

All three of us were alpha together, and their silence gave my words weight.

"I challenge the alphas," Victor said, keeping his voice steady. "Who will stand with me?"

The asshole only needed three voices to start the process.

The word "I" echoed through the room a half dozen times. My heart sank. Our pack had been through so much pain and so much loss, but following Victor now would result in only one thing.

The end of the pack as I remembered it.

CHAPTER
TWELVE

XERXES

The teenage Kitsune lay unconscious on the hospital bed in her room down the hallway from mine. Machines beeped steadily, pumping just enough sedative to keep her out, but not enough to harm the growing fetus inside her.

Right now Sochi was the most valuable commodity in my possession, besides her five month old daughter in the next room. I sighed, scrutinizing every move the nurses I'd personally chosen to tend my prize made. They were in the midst of giving her a sponge bath, but her naked form held no interest for me. Even though she'd already given birth once, her body still held the figure of a young girl. I preferred a woman with a few more curves.

The swell of her lower abdomen had grown rapidly over the last few weeks, and her petite size exacerbated the size of the baby. She was four months along, nearly full-term. Kitsune only had a gestation period of eighteen weeks, so she was very close to delivery.

This second baby would replace Sochi's first daughter, when she aged out at seven months, and keep my research and production moving forward on DNA modifying –giving me the ultimate weapon: Others who could pass for human no matter what test or scan was performed on them. The surrounding Republics would fall like a row of dominos once I could slip a supernatural army across their borders without setting off a single alarm.

Only very young infant Kitsune blood could be manipulated, and because of how young they were, only a small amount of blood could be taken at a time without putting the baby's life in danger.

I refused to lose my investment because of impatience and stupidity.

It'd taken me decades and dozens of scientists to discover infant Kitsune blood held the capacity for such power. These fox shifters were already an endangered species, and I'd unfortunately had to kill several adults and their children to get my hands on Riza and Sochi, daughters of one of their very last Clans. Lucky for me, there was no such thing as a half-blood. Any baby born to a Kitsune was full Kitsune—one of the reasons they weren't completely gone already. One female could restart the entire species if given enough time.

And I'd had two. I should've been able to produce four babies per year each. Eight infants a year, possibly more if multiple in-vitro egg implantations took, providing me with twins or triplets. Multiple births would significantly speed up the production process.

Somehow Riza had slipped out with Manda when she'd freed the fucking Mason wolves. And now everything depended on keeping Sochi healthy and secure. I'd risked the one news cast in hopes of luring Riza back to Savannah. The Kitsune had been told Sochi was dead. Showing her alive and on the SECR newscast had been a calculated risk that so far hadn't panned out.

I left Sochi's room and entered the adjoining room. Bright sunlight streamed in through the large bay window of the old coastal mansion. The happy squeal of a child split the air, and I grimaced at the piercing decibel.

A small woman lay on the floor next to the infant, who could already sit up all by herself in the center of a small blanket. The nursemaid shook a rattle and cooed. The baby laughed and glanced up, catching my gaze—no fear.

The nursemaid gasped and bowed, prostrating herself flat on the floor. Her terror leeched color from her skin. Definitely the response I was more accustomed to receiving.

I approached the baby and lifted her from the floor with my magick, allowing tendrils to tighten gently around her tiny body as I brought her level with my face. She had Sochi's complexion, black hair, and dark brown eyes. Still, it was unsettling to see genuine interest and the complete lack of fear in the infant's eyes. I couldn't remember the last time I'd seen anyone hold my gaze with anything other than fear.

...Actually, I could.

And those hazel eyes were etched into my mind forever. Though the memory was thousands of years old, she had loved me, and I had loved her. Our child would've been the most powerful being in both dimensions –the earth and the Veil. A Lamidae and Lamassu hybrid would've been unstoppable. She and I should've ruled from the stone thrones of Orin; instead, my species interfered and stole her away from me. Her and our unborn child.

My brother sided with the high council, decreeing that I should be imprisoned for life. My brother... My entire race turned on me.

I lost the only woman I'd ever cared about. And with her, my son or daughter. From that moment forward, only revenge and the desire for power kept me pushing forward each and every day.

Within the space of two days, before they could lock me away, I took everything they cared about. Babylon fell to the Horde. My people were massacred with a poison I provided the invading army. In addition to mass genocide of the Lamassu, my brother believed his mate, Rose, and every single one of the Sisters of Lamidae Seers perished at my hand.

Somehow in the midst of my brother's supposed demise, his conniving bitch of a wife escaped my grasp while simultaneously grieving for the loss of her husband —the brother I murdered.

Or so Rose thought.

They'd been instrumental in taking Cera from me. So I'd taken each of them from the other.

"You're going to help make me invisible, little one," I said, keeping my voice deep and even as I suspended the infant in front of me. "And when you're old enough, you will take your place in a bed next to your mother as a priceless brood mare."

CHAPTER
THIRTEEN

TRAVIS

People milled through the room. The tension breathed through me, a living organism that was suffocating. Everyone in the Mason pack was in pain. They'd either lost a mate, a child, or a parent. I remembered the pain when our pack was decimated... when Garrett and I witnessed the slaughter of our parents and pack mates –something no one deserved to live through.

Yet they had, and instead of looking to Charlie for guidance, they were being led astray by a slighted, power-hungry man who thought the best way to survive was to join an enemy that killed for the joy of killing.

I couldn't imagine a universe where Xerxes Hilah would ever choose to help someone other than himself. He was collecting supernaturals. Those who didn't join willingly were killed. It'd been going on for decades, and for decades, the Mason pack had led the charge to help free Lycans and other supernaturals from intolerant Republics. Sanctuary was home to dozens of refugees. Rose took them in and protected them as long as they worked together to keep Sanctuary safe in return.

"A formal challenge has been issued. Law states that before the next sun rises, one of you will fight Victor," said a large male in the background. I recognized him from earlier. Charlie had called him Crawley.

I met Garrett's gaze briefly, and he nodded. No question as to who would fight. His gunshot wound was still healing. The fight with Victor fell squarely on my shoulders, and I was more than willing to wipe the floor with the self-serving asshole. These people rallying around him didn't have a clue what they were signing on for.

"The fight will be mine. My brother was wounded in the attack."

Crawley dipped his chin, acknowledging my statement.

Murmurs filtered through the room. Some followed Victor out of the room, and others stayed, showing their support for Charlie. But the pack was evenly split down the middle. Putting them back together as one unit would probably be next to impossible without losing a few in the process.

For Charlie's sake, I hoped that wouldn't be the case. But the realist in me knew we had more trials ahead than any of us wanted to admit.

"There shouldn't be a fight," Charlie said, her voice flat and without emotion. "They are my mates. The line passed to me. You are defying my father's wishes and insulting both my mates."

I reached to touch Charlie's shoulder. She didn't flinch, but she didn't lean toward my assurance, either. Fury burned in her soul. She needed to say her piece, and I wouldn't deny her that moment, though I knew it wouldn't change the outcome of this evening.

"You spout on about law, Crawley, but you've never respected it. My father took you in when you had nothing. Made you family. And this is the thanks I get. I watched Xerxes murder my parents, and suddenly, you and others are more than willing to join forces with a coward. A coward who wants us to bow to the very enemy who has hunted and murdered our kind mercilessly."

Crawley crossed his arms over his chest, but didn't speak. "The fight begins at dusk," he said before ducking out of the room with the others who followed Victor.

THE SUN SET over a small group of trees behind the lodge. The prairie on either side of the oaks burned red with colors of the sunset, blanketing the hills, grass, and low-growing shrubs with gorgeous jewel tones.

The pack was assembling around an open field a dozen yards or so from the back door. Victor was strutting up and down the line of his supporters, shouting and cursing the weaknesses of Charlie. That outsiders shouldn't lead this family. That he was truly the next in line for alpha and they were right to support a man who would make sure the pack thrived and stayed safe from harm.

Bull-Fucking-Shit. He was going to lead them to

slaughter if I didn't stop him dead in his tracks. My only hesitation was how to win this fight without killing him. I didn't want one of my first acts as an alpha to be offing Charlie's uncle. Though I would do whatever became necessary.

Garrett stepped up behind me, and Charlie positioned herself on my right.

"You don't have to do this. I can call this whole thing off. I'm alpha by right. They have to listen to me," Charlie said, her voice calm and low to avoid being overheard. Still, the words were on the wind, and any Lycan worth his fur could eavesdrop if they really wanted to.

"It won't stop if this doesn't happen," Garrett said before I could speak up.

"I know." The finality in her voice tightened the barbed wire already twisting itself around my heart. Charlie loved this pack. It was killing her to see it so divided. To see so many who said they were loyal to her parents pull away was breaking her very strong heart.

"We're going to get there, Charlie. I promise. Just give it a little time. The pack has been through so much loss. There's going to be unrest. Blame. Hatred, even."

She nodded and leaned her head against my upper arm. "Please be careful. I can't lose you. Either of you."

I turned, pulling her flush to my chest. Garrett moved to stand behind her, and we embraced, both of us placing a kiss on top of her head. Her body trembled between us, but she didn't break. Not a single tear wet my shirt.

"You won't lose us."

"Victor can't win," she murmured. "But..."

"I'll do my best not to kill him, love," I answered,

placing another quick kiss on her forehead before pulling away, leaving her alone in my brother's embrace.

I would do my best. But if he gave me no choice, this would be the last sunset he ever witnessed.

I pulled off my shirt and tossed it to the ground before I stepped inside the ring where Victor was continuing to 'promote' his way as the only option. The comments and ugliness brought out the worst in me, and my wolf strained against my consciousness. Violent urges, most of which included ripping Victor's head from his shoulders, filtered through my mind. I'd promised to try and avoid carnage, but if he didn't shut the fuck up soon, I would have a hard time keeping my word.

"Put your fight where your mouth is, Victor. Or is talking all you're good at?" A low hum started around the ring of pack members. Victor turned to me and glared. If looks could kill, my brains would've been splattered all over the ground while he danced delightedly on my remains. Still I kept prodding. "Not only are you disrespecting and trying to break from your pack alphas, you're trying to get every last one of the pack killed in the process. I wonder how many will thank you for your cowardice on their way to the afterlife?"

He charged, and it was on.

His shoulder slammed into my stomach, but I caught his hips and used his own momentum to flip him over my shoulder. My back slammed against the grass, but he hit the ground with an *ooof* that made my bones cringe in sympathy.

I rolled away as he climbed to his feet again.

Shouts of encouragement to rip off my head or teach

me a lesson were echoed around the circle of angry Lycans. Those on my side were silent, like Charlie, who stood stoically next to Garrett. Neither of their faces read worry.

Both knew my capabilities. They were just waiting for me to finish it.

He moved to the left.

I blocked and moved forward, but he pivoted at the last second and hit me with a mean right cross. Pain surged through my jaw, and I could've sworn a few teeth moved inside my mouth.

Sonofabitch.

Cheers went up from his side of the ring.

I lunged after his retreating form, knocking him to the ground and landing squarely on top of his chest. He may have gotten a good hit in, but it would take more than one solid punch to throw this fight in his favor.

CHAPTER

FOURTEEN

CHARLIE

I'd never seen such a nasty fight. Victor had connected a few more good swings, but Travis wasn't even breathing hard yet. Though Victor wasn't old by Lycan standards, he wasn't used to tumbling around a fight ring, either. Inversely, Travis was decades younger and a trained fighter.

Victor had always been a thorn in my father's side. When he caused more turmoil than normal, Dad reminded me that Victor was family. Still, I never thought he would take his pettiness and desire for power this far.

I could still hear my father's last words. *"Please, kill me and let my family and pack go. They will stop coming into the SECR. They'll disappear, and you'll never see them again."* He'd been willing to sacrifice everything he believed in to save us both. Xerxes hadn't cared. And neither did my uncle, but through everything, I knew my father would still want me to protect Victor. *"Be the bigger person"* he used to say.

The pain of watching Xerxes murder my mother and father in front of me haunted my dreams. But I could not allow Victor to pull the pack toward the same fate.

Travis wouldn't let him.

My mate would not fail me. I only hoped he could do so without taking Victor's life. He was my uncle... and enough of the pack had died already this year.

As the sun drifted lower and the red-orange glow faded to black, the large spotlights on the back of the lodge turned on, and their wash of glaring white light coated all of us.

Victor landed another hard hit to Travis' ribs, and I winced, turning away from the ring for a moment. Garrett stood a few feet to my right, his focus totally on his brother, as was everyone else's except Dean; he had somehow moved around the circle to stand right next to me.

Before I could get a word out, he had a handful of my hair and a knife to my throat.

The din of the pack shouting and screaming at Travis and Victor stopped as if someone had frozen time. I wrenched in Dean's grip, but the knife pressed harder, and a warm trickle of liquid ran down my neck, wetting the front of my shirt.

A roar unlike anything I'd ever heard split the night, and I was knocked to the ground as a huge wolf threw itself against Dean. A terrified scream came from the young male, and then silence hung heavy in the air. Gurgling noises came from beneath the wolf's massive jaws, and blood stained the grass around them. The wolf bit down hard, and everyone in the field heard the snap of Dean's neck. Then the animal wrenched its head back, ripping the young man's neck to shreds.

The knife Dean had held to my neck lay a few inches from his twitching fingers. My stomach turned as I crawled away from him, but I refused to vomit in front of my pack. The traitor had tried to kill me in front of everyone.

Travis and Victor stood motionless in the center of the circle. My gaze sought Garrett's face in the crowd, but my nose told me my mate was right before me, taking vengeance on my would-be murderer.

I may not have agreed with how the execution was performed, but the outcome would've been the same in the end. Dean's offense was an automatic death sentence. What he thought he was accomplishing by trying to kill me in front of the pack eluded my reasoning capabilities.

The wolf swung its head, meeting my gaze.

"It is done, Garrett."

He stepped away from the body and shifted into human form. His face was covered in Dean's blood, and I mourned the loss of another pack mate, though felt secretly relieved my hand hadn't carried out his death.

Garrett had sacrificed for me, taking on that weight and the anger that would follow. Surprisingly enough, no one spoke against him as he walked to my side, his bare skin glistening in the harsh light of the bright outdoor bulbs.

"Please forgive me for not getting to him before he

raised his weapon." Garrett knelt before me, bowing his head.

"There is nothing to forgive. He sealed his fate the moment his weapon touched my skin." I spoke slowly and clearly, allowing my voice to carry across the field. No one else moved or spoke. Not even Victor broke the moment, though I wondered if he were in on Dean's plot.

No one was allowed to attack an alpha female and live. Millennia of tradition and law decreed it one of the most heinous crimes a Lycan could commit. To hurt an alpha's Fated mate was seen as an offense to the goddesses of Fate themselves. It was unforgivable.

Bending slightly, I kissed the top of Garrett's head, sanctioning his actions and ending any dispute another pack member might have had with the execution. As much dissension as I could feel in the air, not a single person disagreed with Garrett's swift justice.

Dean's wife stood apart from the rest of the group, quiet and resigned. They hadn't been Fated mates and had no children, but they'd been married at least five years, and she was a kind woman and a loyal member of the pack.

My heart hurt for her loss. Even love without Fate was a powerful thing. When life stretched over centuries, having a friend and lover could mean the difference between sanity and insanity.

Garrett stood and touched the already healing cut on my neck. I looked down to see several crimson streaks across my breasts where blood had trailed. My shirt was stained as well.

"It's not bleeding. I'll be fine. Go get some new clothes

from my bedroom. I'm going to go clean up in the kitchen really quick," I said, keeping my voice low. Out of the corner of my eye, I saw Travis' large body stalking across the field toward me. "This nonsense can wait. Let us tend to you," he said.

I shook my head, but Victor spoke before I could.

"Looking for an excuse to get out of your ass-whooping, youngster?"

A growl rumbled in Travis' throat, but he kept his focus on me. They both were. Garrett hadn't budged from his spot next to me, standing in all his glory in front of the entire pack.

No Lycan was shy about being nude in front of others, but I preferred not to share the view with other females if it wasn't necessary.

I turned, seeking Crawley out of the crowd of faces. "The fight will cease until my mate and I clean up and return to the circle."

Crawley nodded, taking up a protective stance next to Travis, putting himself between my mate and Victor. The rest of the pack silently dipped their heads, bowing to my wish. Even if they were against the three of us, pack honor would protect Travis. The group as a whole would kill another traitor, if one showed.

"Remove the body from the challenge site," I stated loudly as I walked toward the lodge with Garrett, not caring who carried out the order. Scurrying footsteps behind me and whispers faded into the night as Garrett opened the back door and I stepped through. He turned for the stairs, and I made my way across the living area into the kitchen, eager to rinse the blood from my skin.

CHAPTER
FIFTEEN

GARRETT

I sucked in a deep breath as I yanked on a pair of jeans. Everything had happened so quickly. So instinctually. If I hadn't lunged when I did, Charlotte could've been killed. The scent of her blood on the air had roused my beast, and I'd killed the bastard without thinking twice.

Killing a pack member the day I claimed to be one of their alphas was not the best way to curry favor, but as Charlotte said... the male had sealed his fate when he spilled her blood. Hurting a woman was a grievous act; hurting a female Fated mate was a banishable offense, but hurting a Fated alpha female... there was no returning from that crime. If not my hand, Charlotte's would've been forced to execute him herself.

At least I'd been able to spare her that wound. Her pack's hatred would focus on me instead of her.

I was proud. She'd handled the entire incident well.

Calm. Collected. She was a true alpha, caring so deeply for her pack that the death of the would-be assassin wounded her. I'd seen her pain reflected in her eyes when my wolf had looked up. She hurt for him. Grieved for his loss even while she knew it was necessary.

The other members of the pack were so blinded by their loss and pain they couldn't see the wonderful leader they had. They couldn't see she would give anything to protect them. She'd almost given her life in Savannah. They continued to be angry, forgetting so quickly everything that'd been taken from her as well. They weren't alone in their pain, but they refused to acknowledge hers.

There wasn't a Lycan left alive whom death hadn't touched in some way. Instead of pulling together, many packs had disintegrated into the aether like mine and Travis'. We'd lost track of each other for decades. Joined the military. Killed for killing's sake. Buried the desire for revenge down so hard that it became easy to not feel anything.

Were it not for Charlotte's pain, I wouldn't have considered feeling remorse for my quick decision. I still felt none over the younger male's death.

Nothing.

I'd ripped his throat out because he threatened the life of my mate. That was reason enough for my wolf and reason enough for me.

She didn't judge or condemn me. I'd done nothing our laws didn't uphold. Only my method had been cruel, seeking to cause pain instead of merely providing justice.

I wondered if my brother would make the same choice when he finished the challenge fight.

Wincing as I pulled on a fresh shirt, I rubbed my fingers over the healing bullet hole in my chest. The nearly fatal wound was well on its way to disappearing, but it would be several days before all of the scar tissue was replaced by new growth; until then, it would ache just like a mortal's wound.

Her footsteps downstairs in the kitchen were headed for the back door. I left the bedroom, hurrying down the stairs. We joined paths at the door and walked quietly back to the challenge circle. Everyone waited until Charlotte nodded.

Victor was the first to lunge, but it was not to his advantage. Travis was using the older Lycan's confidence against him, wearing his stamina down slowly with each concerted attack. Here and there, my brother allowed Victor to land a blow, but I was the only one who knew they were strategic moves to keep Victor thinking he had a fighting chance. If the fight didn't stretch out long enough, the pack might not accept the outcome.

Enough members stood against Charlotte to swing a vote against her if they were pushed to that avenue. Travis winning this fight was only part of claiming alpha status of the pack. They had to believe he earned it, not that he merely took it from a less skilled opponent.

Hand to hand combat came naturally to us both. We'd spent decades fighting for one army or another, never the same army and never caring who we were killing as long as we were allowed to spill blood. Our stories were eerily similar and identically as gruesome.

Rose had invited us both to Sanctuary, and the mix-mashed pack that resided there had accepted us both for as long as we wished to stay.

We were willing to move now because both of us knew Charlotte was our future and her heart was planted firmly in Ada. Even though we would leave friends behind, neither of us expected her to give up on her pack. No true alpha would, and she was as strong and as stubborn as they came.

She winced at my side. Victor landed yet another punishing blow to Travis' stomach. I didn't envy his place, but at the same time, I wished that the draw for the challenge hadn't been automatically placed on his shoulders because of my injury. He always seemed to end up bearing the brunt of each situation we were thrust into.

I wrapped my hand around Charlotte's small fingers and squeezed gently. "He's winning," I whispered.

She snorted a small puff of air, making her lack of belief obvious.

But I was pleased. If he was fooling his mate, he was fooling the rest of the pack, too. Sure enough, a few moments later Travis landed a punch that sent Victor sailing through the air to land on the hard ground with heavy thud. A gasp of surprise rolled through the pack, and many who had been on Victor's side were beginning to notice the tide turning. Blow after blow from Travis sent Victor careening from one side of the circle to the other.

Once the onslaught started, he didn't let up until he was sitting on Victor's chest, pummeling the coward's face into a bloody mess.

Without warning, he stopped, stood, and nodded his

head toward Crawley. The pack fell silent, and Travis spoke slowly.

"There will not be another death tonight. If Victor withdraws his challenge, he may remain part of the pack. As well as those of you that stood with him."

The silence grew until the only thing any of us could hear was the wind in the grass and everyone's pounding heartbeat—including Victor's.

"I withdraw," moaned the beaten man on the ground.

A few people moved forward to pick up Victor, and several others offered clean towels to Travis, but he ignored them, making his way straight to us.

"Thank you," Charlotte whispered.

"This one pass was for you, my love," he said.

She squeezed my hand and nodded, understanding that while he would keep his word, he would not grant a second pardon to the man who had likely orchestrated the attack on our bedroom as well as Dean's personal attempt on her life.

The bright lights were switched off, and the field faded into the blackness of the moonless night. Clouds blocked out any natural moonlight. We could see without it, but Lycans drew comfort from the moon. Our shifting had nothing to do with its rise and fall like many human stories claimed, but we revered it as a memorial to the gate home into the Veil. It was a reminder that a place existed where we didn't have to hide our true nature, where we had once been a powerful and free people.

When we chose to shift during a full moon, it was to grieve. Our joined howls on those nights were a chorus lamenting our lost home. At least that's how I remembered my parents explaining our pack's tradition before the Riots.

No one at Sanctuary observed it, but then... Travis and I were the only remaining descendants of the McLennon pack. Even though I couldn't see it, the full moon behind the thick black clouds called to my soul.

For me, over the years it'd changed into a memorial of my lost parents. Of the pack family I grew up without.

"Wait." I pulled Charlotte backward, and she glanced at me with confusion. Travis halted his steps and turned to face me. "The moon is full."

Her brows scrunched together, but Travis nodded, understanding.

"Everyone return to the field," he called out, his voice booming with the authority and power of an alpha. Everyone hurried to follow his direction, and someone flipped the switch on the bright porch lights. "No, turn those off," he bellowed out. They complied immediately, and the field once again fell into a thick darkness.

"Garrett, you speak for us," Travis said, loud enough for everyone hear so they would know it was me speaking.

"Lycans, like all other supernaturals, came from the Veil. We were chased into this dimension by the Incanti Drakonae. They slaughtered thousands. When my father's clan came here, they would shift and howl every full moon to remember their home. To cry for those who were lost and didn't make it through the portal to safety. This pack has suffered such loss. Such pain. To honor those who are no longer with us, I ask that you shift with me and remember them."

I took a deep breath and continued. "It is not shameful to miss our loved ones. I know Travis and I are strangers to you. I know we came in suddenly and claimed Charlotte as our Fated mate and, with it, alpha status in your lives, but you are not alone in your losses. My brother and I lost our whole pack shortly after the Riots started. No one but us remain of the McLennons. But you... you still have many loved ones left to treasure. You still have a pack. Don't forget that."

Charlotte squeezed my hand before releasing it. A moment later, she'd stripped every stitch of clothing from her body, and I watched in awe as she shifted into a beautiful silver wolf. Travis was seconds behind her. Within minutes, everyone had stripped and shifted into their wolf form, even the children who had been hiding behind their parents.

Even Victor.

Peeling off my clothes again, I joined them, feeling a sense of peace as a cloud moved aside, showing the full and stunningly beautiful white moon hanging above us.

My howl started the chorus, and I hoped it was the first step toward repairing the wounds that were tearing this pack apart, but the realist inside me knew the fight for this pack wasn't nearly over.

CHAPTER SIXTEEN

XERXES

The screen on the wall beeped, signaling that my handprint had been confirmed. The whole Whitemarsh Mansion had been outfitted in the most state-of-the-art security system money could buy. Each section and hallway had security checkpoints that required biometric scans to unlock doors and enter. And the laboratory I'd had custom built beneath the mansion was more secure than an army base.

The upper levels where I lived, along with Sochi and her infant daughter, could be accessed by any of my Lycan soldiers and Djinn slaves. But the lab was only accessible by me and a select few. Most of the scientists I'd abducted to run the project ate, slept, and worked around the clock, reminded that they would never see their home or family again if they didn't succeed.

Of course I never shared that I had no intention of ever returning them to their homes alive or that I had killed their families so that no one on the outside was looking for them –would ever look for them.

Loose strings weren't tidy. And I liked my world to be very tidy. Another reason I'd sent Martin to try and lure in the crippled Mason pack. If I could get a few soldiers from them, killing the rest wouldn't be as wasteful, though I was perfectly willing to allow Martin to kill them all. He'd taken most of his pack with him—all trained soldiers. All good killers. All loyal to me.

Martin called his group 'the shadow unit.' They took care of anything I asked without being seen or heard.

Which was good. The less humans looked into the shadows to explain strange events, the better. The shadows were mine, but I wouldn't be staying in them for much longer.

The door ahead of me buzzed and slid to the side. I walked into a quiet laboratory. No one made eye contact as I strolled up and down the counters. Several Lycan guards stood stoically against the far wall of the room, making sure the humans behaved themselves.

The door at the far end of the room buzzed and opened. I glanced that way and smiled when Manda entered.

Her eyes widened as they settled on me, and her feet stalled. But my attention was only on the red folder clutched in her white-knuckled hands.

"Well?" I asked after she stood there a few seconds past shocked.

"The scanning equipment is fully functional again, and the test subjects are all scanning positive for human DNA only."

My chest swelled, and I nearly grinned from ear to ear. "Excellent. Show me," I said, waving toward the door she'd entered through.

She nodded and turned quickly, pivoting on a heel and pressing her hand against the biometric screen next to the door. A red line moved from top to bottom, and it beeped, authorizing her entry into the second part of the laboratory.

The fluorescent lights buzzed in the background, but my focus was only on the man in the white lab coat holding one of the WR's portable biometric scanners. The Lycan in front of him stood patiently as the device scanned and mapped his eye. Humans learned shortly after the Riots that all "Others", as they like to call us, had anomalies within their irises that humans didn't possess. Mostly because our eyes often changed when we accessed our powers or abilities. In the case of Lycans, glowing and color change were definite anomalies that would trigger a negative scan, whether the ability was actively in use or not.

"Has the serum only been tested on Lycans?"

"Yes," Manda answered, careful to stay just outside of arm's length.

Not that it would save her if I wanted to grab her, but psychologically, people felt safer if they thought you couldn't reach them. At this moment, she was off the hook. I had no interest in her. Only in moving forward with the tests.

I turned to the man in the lab coat holding the scanner. "Dose her," I ordered, gesturing to Manda.

A gasp slipped from her mouth, but she didn't

breathe a word of objection. It was a shame. Punishing her for misbehavior was a highlight for me. Although I was still peeved about losing whoever it was who had come out of that last *quppa* box. No one had been able to track her down and nothing about an old Persian woman had come up on any of the local radars.

Although, she may have hightailed it back to the Middle East. It would make sense for her to go home. Nothing in North America would be familiar to her. But technology was everywhere, as well as back in the lands she would call home. Ultimately, my people would locate her.

Only a matter of time. Then I just had to trap her.

The lab coat walked to a refrigerated storage locker across the room and pulled out a small vial. He picked up a syringe from a counter on his way back and approached me and Manda. His pulse was erratic, but he didn't question me. None of them did.

He filled the syringe with the pink liquid from the vial. Then he tugged the shoulder of Manda's sweater down, exposing her upper arm, and jabbed.

Manda jerked and winced as he shot the large dose of serum into her body.

"How long does it take?" I asked the man.

"Not long." He held up the scanner and took a quick reading of one of her eyes. The scanner buzzed, and the screen turned red, alerting to her non-human status. He showed me the negative screen, and I glared.

"How long?"

"Sorry, sir. Should be nearly immediate." A light sheen of sweat had broken out across the lab tech's forehead. His heart raced in his chest, thumping rather loudly against his ribs. He held up the scanner again. This time it chirped, and the screen flashed green. POSITIVE.

Manda scanned as a human.

"It's permanent?"

"As far as we can tell. The serum has not degraded inside the Lycans in the first test group. Their DNA is stable and permanently mutated to include the Kitsune strands from the serum. It shows no signs of destabilizing."

"Excellent." This was the best news I'd had in years. "Monitor them over the next twenty-four hours. And, Manda, bring in twenty more Lycans and that many Djinn by the end of the day to be injected. I want at least a hundred soldiers passing that scan by the end of the week."

"Yes, sir."

CHAPTER SEVENTEEN

CHARLIE

Waking up next to my mates? Best feeling in the world. Even after everything that happened the night before, these two men stood by me, fought for me, and cried with me for the atrocities and losses my pack family had endured. The speech Garrett made after the challenge fight eliminated any inkling of doubt that may have lingered in my mind about them wanting me to leave Ada and move to Sanctuary with them.

They were here for me. For the pack. It was their pack now, too.

I slithered out from between their arms and legs and rummaged through my dresser until I found a pair of panties, shorts, and a tank top. Hopefully, today would be a new beginning.

And the first thing I wanted to start with was some breakfast.

"Charlotte…" Garrett growled from the bed, stretching his long legs past the foot of my queen-sized bed. It was amazing that the three of us managed to stay on the bed at all. A bigger bed definitely needed to move to the top of the shopping list.

"I'm going down to make some breakfast. I'll be back in a few. Just stay here," I said, walking toward him. I leaned down and gave him a quick peck on the lips before leaving the room and heading for the kitchen.

Soon I had a tray heaped with food—eggs, bacon, buttered toast, and three glasses of juice. Plenty of food for all of us.

Footsteps caught my attention, and I glanced behind me. Kara entered the kitchen and leaned against the counter a few feet away.

"Morning," I said.

She scoffed and moved, blocking me as I tried to maneuver around the island with my tray.

"I don't want to argue again, Kara. Please move."

"Bitch," she hissed.

My hackles raised, but she was still blocking my exit, and I'd rather not have a knockdown, drag out fight in the middle of the lodge kitchen. Actually, I'd rather not fight with Kara at all, but she seemed to be pushing for one.

"It's your fault my mate is dead. It's your fault Dean is dead. And your fault everything in this pack is falling to pieces. Victor is trying to save what little is left, and you just want to keep pulling us down until we all drown with you."

Shit. The wild look in her eyes made my heart thump hard against my ribcage. She was a loaded side of crazy.

"We need to be on the winning side. Not the losing side. Do you want all of us to die?"

I put the breakfast tray down on the counter. "Look, Kara—"

She lunged, taking me by surprise and knocking me to the floor. A second later, a flash of metal passed through my peripheral vision, and an intense burn shot through my side.

"Kara!" I coughed, finding it difficult to draw a breath.

I yanked her hand back, and the bloody knife came with it. The woman had stabbed me with a fucking steak knife. "Why?"

She screamed and growled and thrust her weight at me again. I narrowly dodged another stab, and we rolled on the floor. She gasped, and I heard a gurgle in her breath.

Where was the knife?

Tension melted out of her body, and she became nothing more than a limp corpse. Her heart had slowed considerably, and blood poured from a wound in her neck, quickly coating every inch of the tile floor around us. She wasn't dead yet, but she would be. Neither of my mates would let her regenerate.

Footsteps pounded through the lodge. Garrett and Travis burst through the open doorway, yanking her semi-lifeless body from atop me. I sucked in a painful breath. Before I could speak, Travis had already snapped her neck.

Garrett lifted me from the floor and shoved his way

through the people who'd heard the fight and come running. I coughed, desperately gasping for air. My wound was bad, but it would start to heal in a few minutes. Right now, I was choking on my own blood.

I could hear Travis' booming, angry voice downstairs as Garrett carried me up. Besides my pain, all I could think about was that another pack member was dead. Xerxes had cost our pack another life. In less than twenty-four hours, two people had tried to kill me and two people had lost their lives because of it.

Fuck. Fuck. Fuck.

I was doing everything my parents would want me to do, but nothing was going as it should. It was Xerxes and Victor and that bastard of an emissary. He was in on this whole thing somehow. I just didn't know how yet.

"We can't let you out of our sight for even a moment, can we?" Garrett whispered into my ear as he laid me down gently on my bed.

"I was just cooking breakfast. It-I-she..."

"Shhh. It's okay, Charlotte. We are going to get through this with you. I promise."

"She's dead," I sobbed as the shock of what happened finally wore off. "How many of my people have to die?"

"Packs survive because they are united, Charlie," Travis said, entering the bedroom and closing the door behind him. "This pack is divided. Hopefully, there will be no more deaths, but I think an ultimatum should be given. Those who wish to leave Ada should be given that option. Perhaps all of the problems will walk out the door."

"They'll die. I can't let them go to their deaths. I don't

understand. Why. Can't. They. See. It's. A. Lie?" My sobs chopped my sentences into single word chunks.

"Some people refuse to see. Grief blinds them to the obvious," Garrett answered.

I breathed slowly. The pain was fading a little at a time, but at least I didn't feel as though I was drowning any longer. Garrett wiped my face with a washcloth, hopefully removing the last traces of the blood I'd been coughing up.

"You and I know Xerxes is a liar. That that Martin guy has no intention of letting the pack *live* in peace. They are looking for recruits. It's why we've been sneaking into the SECR and other Republics for decades. We are helping people get away from Xerxes. How did they forget that?"

"Pain makes you consider things as options that were unthinkable before," Travis stated, making me wonder how many unthinkable things he and his brother had suffered through or committed themselves. The more I learned about them both, the more my heart broke for them. For the life they led without a family. Without each other. My life hadn't been perfect, but at least I hadn't lost my parents and pack. I truly had been one of the lucky ones.

"What's going on downstairs?"

"Surprisingly, Crawley is maintaining decent order. We may have had a rocky start with him the other night, but I think he might be decent beta material."

I nodded. Crawley was a pain in the ass, but once you had his loyalty, you had it. If he was helping keep everyone calm downstairs, he was most certainly on our side now.

"He's a good man. Just likes to know he's backing the right horse, so to speak," I said softly. "He must've made his choice."

"What?" Travis asked. "That we're the right horse?"

I nodded. "He's very loyal once he's chosen sides. If he's on ours, he won't switch. I can guarantee it. Your fight, Travis, and your speech, Garrett, turned a lot of heads. They might not be showing it in front of Victor, but you both made a huge difference. As much as I hated the challenge fight, it was the right move to make."

"At least they are taking our claim seriously," Travis added.

His brother grunted and then turned his attention back to me. "Do you feel up to going back downstairs?" Garrett asked, holding out a fresh t-shirt he'd snagged from the dresser.

I nodded. He wasn't the only one who could hear the rumblings from the angry pack members who had yet to be swayed to our side. Just because Victor had withdrawn his challenge didn't mean the unrest he'd caused had vanished.

Now there were two deaths to account for.

CHAPTER
EIGHTEEN

TRAVIS

The sound of Victor's opinions floated to meet my ears as I followed Garrett down the stairs. He was carrying Charlie, refusing to let her walk, even though she was arguing that her wound had healed enough and that she wasn't an invalid.

It would've been amusing was I not worried about corralling a pack full of crazy in the living room. I wished desperately for Charlie's blessing to snap another neck—Victor's. Eliminating him would wash most of the negativity right out of this lodge. He was an instigator. A pot stirrer. I was rapidly growing to despise him.

Nix that. I already despised him. What I really wanted to do was beat the shit out of him again and then pull his traitorous tongue through the hole I would carve in his throat. A fitting and painful death for a man determined to sell out his pack to the most heinous, evil man who ever walked the face of the earth.

"Silence!" I shouted, enjoying the slight reverb in my voice as it echoed through the large living area. Everyone's mouth snapped shut, except for Victor.

"These men don't belong. Look how easily they kill. Charlie should leave with them. They are outsiders just trying to take over a pack because they lost their own." His voice carried on and on until the beast inside me snapped.

I stalked up to him, nearly pressed my face to his, and snarled. "You are alive because I spared you. Because Charlie, even after everything you've done to undermine her, begged me not to kill you. You deserve nothing from her or from this pack. It. Is. Not. Yours. End of story. If you or anyone else feels the need to continue to question Charlie's, mine, or Garrett's leadership qualities, you are free to leave immediately. No questions asked. Just get out and don't come back."

Victor sneered back at me, and I nearly smiled; instead, only the very corner of one side of my mouth turned up.

"I promised not to kill you during the challenge fight, but that promise ended as soon as we walked off the field that night. I'm just waiting for the next time you screw yourself over so I can yank that traitorous heart right out of your chest. As for the rest of you, make your choice." I gestured to everyone standing around the outside of the great room. "We answered the call of our Fated mate. This pack meant nothing to us until we met Charlie. Charlie is your alpha, but so are we. This pack is our family now as much as it is hers. We care about each and every one just like she does."

"You should go. All three of you," another shouted from the back of the room.

A chorus of *yes* filled the room, pissing me off a little more. Here was a pack on the verge of collapsing, and they were so blinded by grief and fear that they would rather follow the man who would lead them to their deaths than an alpha Fated by the gods.

"You will stop this nonsense and whining!" My voice boomed, taking on a larger-than-life quality, and the room fell silent. "You bitch and moan like pack toddlers, complaining that life isn't fair. Guess what? In case you hadn't noticed, you aren't the only one life has shitted on!"

Several people dropped to their knees and bowed their heads, showing their submission to my alpha status immediately, but quite a few shook their heads, refusing to answer the call of the magick I knew was tugging at their soul. I remembered the feeling of belonging to a pack. The force of the connection I'd had with my father. It was like nothing else on the planet.

Their wolves should want it. Desire it above everything else.

Victor stepped forward, a smug, confident smirk spreading across his face.

CHAPTER
NINETEEN

CHARLIE

My soul basked in the love and commitment flowing from Travis. He'd given the group his best shot, but they just wouldn't accept him. Victor kept stirring the pot, re-opening old wounds. It wasn't fair. He wouldn't let them move on.

I wished I knew why he wanted to join with Xerxes. What had the monster promised him when no one was listening? What was worth turning over your entire pack to be slaughtered?

Stepping closer to Travis, I slid my hand into his and squeezed, taking solace in the connection that flowed between us. Garrett took the place on my other side, and once again I was sandwiched between them. Didn't bother me. Being between them had turned into my favorite place to be. He took my other hand and held it tightly.

My heart weighed heavy in my chest. I drew comfort

from my connection with Travis and Garrett, but it couldn't shut out the pain that burned in my breast for my two fallen pack members. They were casualties of a war I didn't want to fight.

"You know me." I said staring across the room, connecting with as many pack gazes as I could. "You know my heart cries with yours for each and every loss. Every one of you is my family. I have always been loyal to you. What would my parents think if they could see how you're treating their daughter? The daughter they raised to care more about you than anything else in this world."

I swallowed and took a deep breath. "If you truly do not feel the connection that I do, I will not stay with people who wish me dead and gone. I will not force my love on you. I will go without a word, and you can have Victor and all his promises. Two lives have already been lost, and my heart weeps for each of them. The wounds they inflicted aren't healed yet. The blood they drew from my body still lies fresh on towels in this house. I *feel* their loss," I said, doing my best to hold back the flood of tears.

They were breaking my heart. This pack meant everything to me, and I'd been the cause of not one but two executions in the last twenty-four hours.

It had to stop. If I had to leave the only home I'd ever known, I would.

"You heard her. Speak your wishes now," Victor crowed, stepping forward from the back of the room.

Murmurs of disagreement rumbled through the room. No one stepped forward. Victor was silent for once. His last attempt to strip me of my family had been thwarted by the very people he thought he'd turned against me.

"We will mourn our pack members who thought their only choice was killing me. The dead will be buried and their memory preserved. They were loved. No matter the pain that made them choose ugliness, they are still loved."

Crawley pushed through the crowd and knelt at my feet like a knight from the Middle Ages. He didn't speak. Just waited.

"Crawley," I said, laying my hand on his shoulder. I could feel Travis and Garrett's breath behind me, but neither of them spoke. Crawley had made his fealty public by bowing at the alpha female's feet. It was a custom not unlike the knights in the Middle Ages who pledged to protect and serve the queen of the land. "Please oversee the preparations for Dean and Kara's funeral. I would like to hold that service tonight and send their bodies peacefully into the afterlife. I pray the gods will forgive them their sins as I have already done."

I looked up into the crowd of female faces that were depending on me and my mates to keep them safe; only a handful of males remained. We could do this, right? I wasn't asking too much of Travis and Garrett? As if they'd read my mind and my doubt, their hands settled on each of my shoulders.

"Crawley has shown his loyalty and will officially take the place in the pack as our beta. Follow his direction and prepare the pack for the funeral ceremony. Our mate needs to rest," Travis announced.

Rest? I didn't need to rest. My pack needed me. There

were five males in this lodge who needed to pack their shit and get out. Instead they all stood together in the corner, pouting like puppies who'd lost their toy.

"Later, my love," Travis said, keeping his voice low as he pressed his hand to my lower back and practically shoved me toward the stairs. "They can wait. Let your mates cleanse from you the carnage of today. Let us love your body, mind, and soul, Charlie."

No. That was not what I needed. There was work to be done. They were trying to handle me. But hearing sentiments fall from Travis' lips instead of Garrett's caught me off guard. Travis was always sharper than Garrett. But the softness from him shocked me to silence, probably the result he'd wanted.

"Don't look so surprised, Charlotte," Garrett chuckled. "This is what we've wanted since we met you that first day we came to Ada looking for a dragon."

I remembered that day, too. The way they'd looked at me. The way my body had burned with desire. And the way I'd pushed them away. The pack had needed me more, and they would've been a distraction.

The pack continued to demand my attention, and my mates remained a distraction.

They would always be a distraction, but now it was one I craved more than life. The mating heat that consumed my body had been cooled after our first coupling, so my body had ceased to obsess over them; instead, my heart had taken over that role.

But if I let the bond settle and then lost them, it might destroy me for good.

I'd watched Xerxes' army kill half my pack on the hillside next to Vicksburg Bridge. Watched him murder my parents in front of me. Listened to them choke on their blood as they fought for their last breath.

How much more could I take without breaking?

I kept walking, anyway. And I let my mates guide me up the stairs toward my room.

This was all of me and I was risking it all for them.

CHAPTER
TWENTY

CHARLIE

The scent of male filled my lungs. My naked mates advanced toward me, making the corners of my mouth turn up. Their sleek bodies brought a fire to my belly like nothing else could. I stood silent and clothed as they circled me, prowling like the predators living within them.

Their eyes shone, gleaming with golden flecks as their wolves fought to come forward. Instead, the men won over the beasts, and they both touched me at the same time, sending a shock of electricity tingling across my skin. Our magick melted together like molten steel. We were stronger together as a bonded triad than we'd ever been separately.

I shivered, holding my breath. This was a distraction. Nothing more. I refused to let it be more. Magick be damned.

Travis ran his hands along my torso, taking hold of

my shirt hem and tugging it up slowly, giving me time to raise my arms to accommodate being stripped. Garrett worked the lower half, pulling from my waist downward, until I could feel a cool draft of air across my slick mound. Then his face was there. His warm breath and hot tongue caressed my skin. He licked my slit until my knees buckled. I sucked in a long gasp of air.

Travis caught me in his arms before I collapsed and laid me on the bed behind us.

My eyes closed and I just *felt*. Everything.

Our magick pulsated through the room as our heart rates sped.

Garrett's mouth licked and sucked and brought me right to the edge of an orgasmic precipice, but pulled back at the last second. I groaned, opening my eyes and reaching for his head. But he'd moved out of my grasp.

"I want to feel you come around me, my love," Garrett said.

"And I want those lips on my cock," Travis growled, his voice hitting a low rumble that made my insides melt. "Flip over, love. Up on your knees." Garrett's hands maneuvered my hips, and I rolled, crawling to my knees as Travis moved to sit in front of me, positioning his hard cock only inches from my mouth. It glistened with precum, and I could smell the salty tang of him in the air. I licked my lips then swiped my tongue across his tip.

"Hey there," Travis said, taking my head in his hands and capturing my lips with his. He took a kiss and moaned into my mouth, his deep voice vibrating through me and awakening my body better than any battery operated device ever could.

Garrett's hands closed around my hips, and he lifted me a few inches so that my knees were directly under my body and my ass was high. I shuddered as he licked my slit from behind, fucking my pussy with his tongue. In and out. Deeper and deeper.

"Gods, you taste so good, Charlotte. I won't ever get tired of the taste of your sweet honey on my tongue."

I moaned through Travis' kiss.

He pulled away from my mouth and released my head. "Take me, sweetheart."

Dipping my head, I swirled my tongue around his cock. It was softer than velvet, yet harder than steel. I bobbed lower, taking the tip into my mouth. He threaded his fingers through my hair, pressing me a little lower each time I went down.

My pussy throbbed, hovering on the edge of bliss. Tortured by Garrett's skilled mouth, his fingers, but not his cock. *Fuck.* I wanted his fucking cock inside me. I wanted both of their cocks inside me, coming, filling me up—making me whole.

Wait. No. My body slammed that thought back into the recesses of my mind.

The damn bond was affecting my emotions, weakening my resolve. They did not get to make me whole. They couldn't. Nobody could. I'd lost too much already. I couldn't afford to give away another piece of my soul, only to have Xerxes slice it away as well.

Raising my head, I dropped Travis' cock and turned to look over my shoulder. "Fuck me, now," I growled, letting my magick flare. I could see the glow of my eyes reflected in Garrett's irises.

"With pleasure," he said, grabbing my hips and burying his hard length inside me.

I screamed as the orgasm I'd been chasing crashed around me, pulling my mind one way and sending every synapse of my body careening another. I pulsed around him, and then he began to thrust.

Slow at first.

"Harder," I moaned through gritted teeth.

He complied, and I pushed backward with each movement, finding his rhythm and matching it. As I sunk into the orgasm-induced bliss of being impaled over and over, Travis threaded his fingers into my hair and guided my mouth back to the tip of his cock.

"I'm going to fuck your pretty mouth, Charlie."

I nodded, parting my lips and taking his whole head. Slowly he worked my mouth up and down. Using my tongue to slick his flesh, I slid farther and farther until the tip of his shaft nudged at my throat.

"More, Charlie," he coaxed, pressing my head down.

My body shuddered, hyper-aware of Garrett's cock pumping in and out of my pussy. Slow then fast. Soft then hard. Always changing the pattern. Another orgasm was unfurling within me, warming every nerve ending. I wanted to disappear into it. I wanted them to fuck me until I couldn't feel the pain of what I'd lost. Of what I might lose in the future.

Garrett shouted, slamming deep one more time.

I arched my neck and screamed around Travis' cock as the second orgasm tore through me, shredding what little control I thought I had left. He groaned and tightened his fingers through my hair, pulling me down harder over his cock. His cum shot down my throat, and I took every salty drop.

Garrett's fingers dug into my hips as he jerked and stiffened behind me. His warm seed filled my body.

It didn't work.

I still felt everything

The connection between us tugged at my heart. Those walls needed to be higher. They might be my Fated mates, but I needed to *not* need them. Even though Victor hadn't succeeded during the challenge, it was only a matter of time before he tried again. Or Xerxes found a way to destroy me completely.

My lips smacked as I dropped Travis' cock after licking it clean. Looking up, I caught his gaze and smiled. "Round one was fun. What's the plan for round two?"

The prodding had the desired effect. Travis' gaze narrowed. "As you wish, sweetheart." The snark in his voice promised another solid fucking, but I caught a glimpse of a question.

A question I didn't want to answer. Not right now. Right now I only wanted to fuck.

Turning away from him quickly, I sought Garrett. He stood at the foot of the bed, his cock standing gloriously erect from a nest of dark curls as if he'd hadn't just come. The look on his face said he doubted my request for another go-round, but his cock begged to differ.

And if I had anything to say about it, his cock would win the argument.

"Please."

He nodded and then glanced past me to his brother.

Before I could turn around, Travis had slid forward

on the bed, grabbed me by the waist, lifted me onto his chest, and slammed me straight down on his hard cock, impaling me all the way to my core. Impressive recovery time, even for a Lycan.

I let my head drop backward as a scream caught in my throat. His arms wrapped around my waist, constricting and tightening like a snake until my breasts were crushed against his chest.

"You will not use sex to escape what is bothering you again, Charlie," he whispered into my ear.

I stiffened. *Shit.* "Just fuck me." He could be pissed at me later. Couldn't a woman just get a good fuck? Or was that something the world only offered to men?

The drawer beside my bed scraped open and shut. I turned toward the noise. Garrett held a bottle of arousal lube in his hand. He squirted an overly generous dollop into his palm and then spread it up and down his sheathed cock. *Where the hell did he get a condom?* The latex would protect him from the stimulant in the cream.

I would not be so lucky. That stuff made me more sensitive than gunpowder exposed to a flame thrower. And he had every intention of burying himself in my ass. *Oh, gods!* Punished with my own apparently not-so-secret stash of self-stimulating products.

I wriggled in Travis' hold, anticipating and wanting to escape the torture I knew was coming at the same time. A shiver ran across my skin. I trembled when Garrett slid one of his palms along my hip and down around the curve of one of my ass cheeks.

The tip of his cock grazed the tight rosebud of muscles, and I tensed again. "You're going to let us in,

Charlotte. All the way." His voice deepened on the second statement, letting me know he was talking about more than just the sex.

He pushed a little harder, breeching with just the head of his cock.

I gasped, the warmth of his cock contrasted with the cooling cream he'd spread over it. But the icy sensation only lasted a few seconds before it turned to fire. He drove a little deeper and then stilled, giving me time to adjust to the fullness.

My pussy flexed around Travis' cock, and another orgasm twisted and writhed inside of me, working its way outward with each thrust of their cocks.

Travis pumped slowly, and Garrett joined him, pulling out in rhythm as Travis thrust in.

I moaned, burying my face in Travis' chest. They might be upset with my manipulation of the situation, but I was getting what I wanted. A good, hard fuck.

Then, as if he could read my mind—which he couldn't—Garrett drove deep and hard, speeding his thrusts. Travis matched his pace, and I screamed as the world rushed around me in a brilliant explosion of color. Every muscle in my body contracted at the same time, and I screamed again then growled through the next orgasm and then another. Wave after wave of exquisite, torturous bliss pulled me away from the emotional baggage threatening to drown me.

I flew above it all.

Garrett came first then Travis. A peaceful blanket of exhaustion settled over me. Their hands stroked my body, caressing and rubbing as they moved me to lie between them. Their voices were deep and rolled like the ocean waves of the gulf, lulling me down from the high place they'd sent me.

They had given me what I thought I wanted, but instead turned it into what I didn't even realized I needed.

Both of them made me whole. Not one or the other. Both.

Each was a piece of my soul that I'd been searching the world for all my life.

But I wouldn't accept them, not completely. I couldn't.

It would hurt too much when they were taken. This was as close to heaven as I could allow my heart.

CHAPTER
TWENTY-ONE

XERXES

"How many have been dosed with the serum now?" I asked the tech trembling beside me as I perused the screen of his computer.

"Ninety-seven."

"That's good. But I need more than that. I'll tell Manda to send the rest to you. I want them all dosed before the end of the week. Is that clear?" I asked, lowering my voice.

The man didn't wet himself, but I could tell he was close. Sweat poured from his forehead, running down his temples in rivulets of tortured anxiety. His breathing was rapid and uneven, and his heart rate was all over the place.

"Calm yourself and do your job," I growled. He was a competent scientist, one of the brightest in the field of molecular biology, but he was one of the most nervous humans I'd ever encountered.

"Yes, sir. I'm just... I might not have enough—"

"I'm not going to kill you as long as you do your job." I turned and gazed down at him, meeting his muddy brown gaze. "So fucking suck it up and make it happen!"

His head twitched up and down and then to the side a couple of times before he mumbled a "Yes, sir". Then I stalked out of the room, put my hand against the biometric scanner, and smiled at the sound of the heavy door locking in place behind me.

Two Djinn materialized in the hallway before me. I raised an eyebrow, slightly surprised at their presence. If there were reports, they usually waited for me to get back to my office upstairs.

Both men dropped to one knee, and the closest one spoke. "Sir, forgive the intrusion. There is a group approaching Savannah. We are quite sure it's the Drakonae and the others from before. And..."

Why the fuck would they come back? Unless... I smiled. Perhaps I would recapture Riza after all.

"And what?" I asked, realizing he'd cut himself short.

"Rose Hilah is with them."

A shiver slid over my body, causing the hair on every inch of my skin to stand straight up. Rose hadn't left Sanctuary in over a century. What could possibly have her riled enough to leave her precious town?

The Kitsune?

It had to be. She'd figured out what I was doing and was coming to try and stop me. No fucking chance.

"Put an extra detail on the two Kitsune. I don't want

anyone or anything getting in or out of this house without my permission," I ordered the closest guard. "Then you," I said, gesturing to the second guard, "take me to them. I need to speak with her."

"Yes, sir."

The first man blinked away, disappearing into a wrinkle of space. I stepped closer to the second Djinn. He reached out and touched my arm; I took a breath before time and space folded around us. The vortex swirled, but I was used to it after so many years of traveling through them. The trip didn't turn my stomach any longer or disorient me. In fact, I quite looked forward to the rush.

A second later, I was standing on a hillside overlooking a small farmhouse. Magick rippled through the air like static electricity. Rose appeared shortly, stepping out onto the back porch of the house. She blocked the sun with her hand and peered up the hill to where I was standing next to the Djinn at the tree line.

We hadn't been this close to each other in... thousands of years. She was as heart-stompingly beautiful as the last time I remembered seeing her—shortly after removing my brother from her life. That particular deed would eventually come in handy, but for now, my traitorous asshole of a brother could continue to rot beneath the old city while Rose believed what I wished her to—that her husband, Niram, was dead and gone.

She wasn't my beloved Cera, but Rose certainly stirred my blood with desire. Unfortunately, Hades itself would freeze over before I got the chance to put Rose in a compromising position, especially when she surrounded herself with the rarest and most powerful supernaturals found on earth.

My magick reaffirmed that the Drakonae son of the Blackmoors did indeed travel with her again. *Should've killed him the moment I laid eyes on him back in Orin.* In addition, she had the bloody Gryphon and Phoenix with her. Not that individually I couldn't take them, but with all three of those powerful men at her beck and call, she was untouchable, even for me. Our magick didn't work on each other. If I ever took down Rose Hilah, it would be with a sword forged in Dragon's Breath. Like the sword that fucking Elvin had stabbed me with weeks earlier.

Death had knocked on my door that day, but since then, I'd become more vigilant. They would not take me by surprise again. Knowing they had the swords made them useless. I would never put myself in a vulnerable position again while the weapons remained outside of my possession. In the meantime, I'd lost nearly a dozen Djinn to recovery efforts. When the warrior I sent only seven days ago also failed to return, I knew Rose was either killing or boxing them up for safekeeping. So I'd discontinued the search for now. Risking more of my Djinn warriors to Rose's clutches was foolish...and I was far from foolish.

"What do you want, Rose?" I spoke quietly, allowing my magick to carry my voice down the hillside to her stoic form.

"I've come for the young Kitsune girl," she answered, sending her words on a soft breeze.

I smiled. *One girl.* She didn't know Sochi already had a child. I'd separated the sisters before they'd gotten pregnant. Riza would have no way of knowing Sochi conceived or delivered a baby already.

"You're smart enough to know why I won't give her to you. And why you should want me to keep her." At least now I knew Rose monitored the news stations.

"Then why did you come all the way out here to talk to me? What do you want, Xerxes?"

I shrugged. "It's been a long time, Rose. When my soldiers reported seeing you, I just had to see for myself that the great Rose Hilah left her cave and ventured into the world, leaving her precious Sisters for the first time in over a century. If we didn't want to kill each other, I'd say we should have a drink and celebrate."

Her face tightened, and a frown stretched down the corners of her mouth. Her hatred for me still weighed on her soul, coating the pulses of magick rolling off of her with darkness. Each supernatural had a distinct magickal pattern, like an electromagnetic pulse, that emanated from their body. The stronger the being, the stronger the pulse of magick. Rose and I had two of the strongest wave patterns on the planet, seconded only by a Drakonae.

I raised my hands to waist level and felt the charges in the air. She'd brought very powerful supernaturals with her, but there was a trace signature of another that was no longer with her group. One that was just as powerful as the Gryphon and Phoenix, possibly stronger.

"Who else was with her?" I asked, turning to the silent Djinn soldier at my right.

"Just the Gryphon, Phoenix, and Drakonae, sir," he answered. "We saw no others."

"You're hiding something, Rose," I projected my voice again, allowing magick to carry it to her.

For someone who had come for my Kitsune, she was awfully calm about being confronted... as if there was another plan entirely.

Fuck.

"Take me back to the house now!" I grabbed the Djinn by the arm, and we blinked away, teleporting to the center of my office in the Whitemarsh Mansion.

No alarms.

I opened the door and stepped into the hallway. Bodies littered the floor, but they were all alive. Alive and snoring.

Leaping over several prone soldiers, I shoved my way into Sochi's room. The monitors were off, the bed was empty, and her three nurses lay in a peaceful heap in the corner of the room.

"Fucking, bitch!" I continued through the bedroom and into the infant's nursery. Her nurse lay sleeping in the rocking chair. Hurrying across the room, I peered into the crib and sighed. The baby, as well, slept peacefully, undiscovered during the Siren's little rescue run.

In all of history, Calliope Hart had never helped anyone but herself. How the hell had Rose convinced the selfish bitch to sneak into my home—by herself—and take what belonged to me?

"Sir," the Djinn who'd been with me spoke. "How do we wake them up?"

I scoffed. "We don't. The useless bastards will sleep at least twenty-four hours and then wake up on their own. A Siren's song is irreversible except by the Siren herself."

In old times, an experienced Siren could waylay an entire fleet of ships, lulling the sailors to their deaths on rocky shores and were usually paid to do so by the highest bidder. Calliope had always been one of the most powerful Sirens on earth —and one of the few sirens still known to be alive. Apparently, she hadn't lost her charm in her old age. Except, this time, she'd put down my entire fighting force.

"Bring me a witch," I snarled. If Calliope was truly one of Rose's allies, I would be certain everything and every building were warded to keep her and her ultrasonic song out.

"Should we not go after them first?"

I shook my head. "They won't be there." I turned on my heel and faced the soldier who dared to question me. I grabbed him around the neck with my powers and squeezed. He clutched at the air around his neck and coughed, fear making his eyes bulge. "Don't ever waste time by questioning me again. Do you understand?"

He tried to nod his head.

I released him from my magickal chokehold, and he fell to the floor with a loud thud.

Again, Rose had ruined my plans. Not completely, instead merely setting me back. I still had Sochi's first baby. Her blood would disguise my small army for now, but it would be years before she was mature enough to breed and carry a baby of her own. Meaning I needed to get as many soldiers dosed as possible in the next few months before her blood was useless, including myself.

I would not wait another decade or two to move forward with my plans.

CHAPTER
TWENTY-TWO

TRAVIS

The air outside the lodge was thick with anger and the scent of propane from the torches lit around the burial circle. Two bodies lay in the center of the circle, each with their own pine box. Crawley had spent the entire day making them while the rest of the pack prepared the herbs and items needed for the funeral fire. We didn't burn bodies any more--that was a tradition that stopped hundreds of years ago--but tightly knit packs did still burn incense and herbs on a small fire near the bodies. A sacrifice to call on the gods to lead the fallen souls to the safety of Elysium. Though if it were up to me, I'd cover their coffins with tar and send them on their way to Tartarus—their souls trapped by the tar and never able to escape the pine box holding their bodies.

My mate was more gracious than I and surprisingly more forgiving. She'd insisted on a burial ceremony that gave the deceased the best chance of finding peace. It was what she wanted for her pack most of all, but Garrett and I had already discussed alternatives if peace could not be achieved. We wouldn't force her to leave Ada—it wasn't the Lycan way to force a female into any decision—but we knew it was an option that would continue to arise if this problem with Victor wasn't dealt with swiftly.

So far, he'd given us no reason to eliminate him outright. Instead, he continued to whittle away at the integrity and morale of the pack. Turning one member after another against Charlie. I could smell the disloyalty, anger, and frustration. It was hard to blame them. They'd lost so much when the Djinn had betrayed them. Now two more of their family had turned to murder and paid the ultimate cost—their own lives.

And for what? A man who wanted to feed them straight to the beast we all knew would betray them and most likely kill them.

Xerxes was evil. Angry. And out for blood and power. The only reason he wanted this pack was to harvest the few who would turn away from their freedom and work for him.

In exchange for what?

Not dying. Not having their throat slit.

The hair on the back of my neck stood on end. I stepped into the ring of the funeral circle to stand next to my brother. His proximity protected us both, but the feeling of being stalked did not fade.

Charlie was being hunted by her own. But so were we.

Garrett glanced over to me and nodded to his left. My

gaze traveled the invisible line and noticed Victor standing behind several other pack members.

One of the standing torches marred my view of Victor, but as I focused on him, the words falling from his lips ceased.

Lycans were a species renowned for their hearing. A whisper fifty yards away for us was as clear as two humans speaking to each other across a dining table.

She will pay. Those were the only words I caught before Victor stopped speaking and moved away from the circle.

It was enough to make my heart race and sweat break out on my brow. Muscles throughout my body flexed and released, tensing and readying to attack. I wanted to rip his heart from his chest and tear out his throat with my teeth. My wolf was angry and anxious, a bad combination for any predator.

Several women near the small bonfire in the center of the circle, between the two coffins, began chanting Greek words I'd heard only a few times before the Riots. Afterward, they were a constant drone in the back of my mind. Garrett and I had buried everyone in our pack. Then I'd buried friend after friend through the years. When an unfamiliar Lycan had reached out to me from Sanctuary, offering a place to rest, I'd taken him up on it.

Sanctuary had been just that for me. A place to rest. To repair my shredded soul. And to wash away the years of blood and evil that had stained it. I'd done many things I wasn't proud of to survive or in the name of justice for my kind.

Rose had slowly shown me over the years that

revenge wasn't all it was cracked up to be. She'd lost her husband millennia before I'd been born, but she'd found a way to move on. To put something else before the pain and focus on others.

She couldn't help her husband, so she gave her whole life to these women who needed to be protected. I wasn't privy to all the details about the Sisters of Lamidae, but I knew enough to realize that, in the wrong hands, seers could invariably end the world on this plane of existence. And since returning to the Veil wasn't really an option and hadn't been for a thousand years, Earth was a place we needed to care for and protect.

The chanting from Charlie and several of the other women stopped as they sprinkled the bodies of the dead with freshly ground herbs and spiced oils. Then Crawley closed the lids of the coffins. As he nailed them shut, Charlie moved to stand next to us at the head of the two empty graves waiting for Dean and Kara. The other women moved to various positions around us in the circle of pack and brightly burning torches.

We'd waited until the evening to do the ceremony. Something else Charlie had insisted on. A moon to guide their spirits. It shone brightly above us in the cloudless sky, surrounded by twinkling stars—representations of the souls that had already left this world.

Charlie slipped a hand into mine. Garrett stepped closer and slipped his hand around her other one. Our magick flowed powerfully through our mate bond. I could feel the strength we possessed together. It surprised me that after all this time, Fate would bring

Garrett and I back together this way and seal our bond so permanently.

"On this night, we bid two of our family farewell."

The drone of chanting stopped on all sides.

Charlie huffed through a breath, trying to disguise her emotion, but among sorrow and pain, I could smell anxiety and fear. She didn't trust her pack any more than Garrett and I probably did. Two had tried to kill her already, and a blood uncle continued to plot our demise. Still, she fought for her composure and refused to deny her pack a proper burial.

"They made choices that put them where they are right now. Choices I wish had been different. I would give my life to save my pack. To bring all of my family back that's been lost. In honor of those who were buried without Lycan ritual on the hillside of Vicksburg and those who died in Savannah without a burial at all, tonight we burn enough oil and incense to light their way to the fields of Elysium. May the gods light their path and show them a place where they can find peace."

I waited, sure that someone would speak out and ruin the ceremony. But the rippling anger and discontent simmered beneath a lid of propriety. None spoke against her. Not even a whisper.

It was respectful and honorable.

But the discord was coming. Tentacles of misery crept out from the dark shadows of their souls. This would not be an easy fight or one without more blood spilled.

I just needed to be sure it wasn't Charlie's blood on the ground. Or mine and my brother's. No matter how much she loved this pack, they weren't worth martyring ourselves. I'd learned years ago that death was a useless form of tribute unless those you died for loved you.

There was not much love left in this place, but come hell or high water, Garrett and I would give it everything we had because they were all Charlie had left. We knew firsthand the pain of losing everyone you loved. If we could spare her that pain, we would in a heartbeat. I knew without asking Garrett felt the same way. I'd seen the determined way he rolled his shoulders and held his tongue.

The evil stalking the Mason pack was smart and left no tracks. Until we had Victor lifting his physical hand against her, we couldn't act without betraying her trust—our bond—and he knew it.

CHAPTER
TWENTY-THREE

CHARLIE

Another whole day passed without incident. Victor was minding his manners, or so it seemed. Travis and Garrett were wired, though. We slept quietly together after Dean and Kara's funeral. They held me while I slept, but took turns sleeping themselves. I woke once in the night and saw the moonlight glinting off Garrett's open eyes. He'd turned toward me a second later, no doubt hearing the change in my breathing or the slight rise in my heart rate.

A smile and deep kiss was enough to coax me from Travis' arms. But he was only taking me from his brother so he could take a turn sleeping with me tucked tightly against his body. I wasn't complaining.

I loved being near both of them. Being held, caressed. Loved. It was everything my soul had dreamed of experiencing with one mate. Fate had given me two. But two meant twice the heartache when Xerxes stole them from me. I steeled my heart to the avalanche of emotions threatening to kick in the walls I'd erected to protect myself.

Each touch. Kiss. Look. Everything they did was for me, but all I could see was pain and how much it was going to hurt to lose them. I couldn't love them the way they loved me. Recklessly. Completely. Without hesitation.

The bond flowed between the three of us, bathing me in the constant glow of their feelings for me. Of their hopes and dreams of our future together. A future that Xerxes would invariably steal from me if Victor didn't first. But it didn't matter if the whole pack hated me. I was their alpha. It was my job to love and care for them and make sure they were taken care of first. I came second. My needs, wants, and wishes were at the bottom of the list. They always had been as long as I'd lived. My parents had raised me to put the pack first.

That was why the disloyalty and hatred hurt so much. I'd given everything to these people. To my family. But they were blinded by the same pain I carried in my heart. Pain that had left my eyes wide open but stolen my ability to hope. No obvious way out of this mess existed. I'd tried to show my dedication, my forgiveness to the two pack members who'd tried to assassinate me so Victor could lead them to the slaughter. It wasn't enough. They wanted to follow my uncle to their deaths.

Travis and Garrett were both a walking bundle of sizzling nerves. If they thought I couldn't feel their anxiety and smell the concern seeping from every pore of their body, they were wrong. But I respected them more for staying quiet about it. They were doing their best to help me achieve my goal of keeping the pack safe, no matter how crazy an idea it might be. For that, I would be eternally grateful.

"You need to let your mind rest, Charlie," Travis whispered, his big bass voice rumbling through the air between us.

He used my nickname most of the time, unlike Garrett who always called me Charlotte. Charlie made me feel strong and capable of fighting the war that threatened to swallow us up. Both fed different parts of my soul. Both gave me something I desperately needed, but wouldn't wholly accept.

Even so, I would make my vows to both of them when the sun rose. Crawley had insisted we complete a traditional Lycan marriage ceremony. A decade had passed since the pack had celebrated a wedding, and it would be a nice change from the hell we'd been through lately. I'd agreed totally with him, surprised and pleased with his change of attitude since Travis and Garrett had appointed him their beta. That one choice had changed Crawley from a whining, self-serving jerk into a loyal, steadfast member of our pack.

Our pack. A pack that consisted of Travis, Garrett, myself, and Crawley, for all intents and purposes. Crawley said disloyalty was rampant, though others had not publicly raised their voices against our alpha status, and that many spoke of leaving Ada with Victor permanently.

"Yours doesn't," I finally whispered back.

He sighed like a man who understood why my mind

couldn't rest. Like a man who knew, but wouldn't stop me from trying my damnedest to make this work.

What if I kept pushing and pushing and *I* was the reason I lost these two perfect mates Fate had delivered to my doorstep? Was I so blind that I would waste this opportunity? An opportunity not every Lycan was granted. A chance to be so connected to another that you could feel their essence inside you. A chance to have a family. There was a time when that had been all I dwelled on.

But it seemed so small in comparison to the evils out in the world. The evils that could snuff out everything I cared about with one little breath.

"Are you concerned about the vows we take tomorrow?" Travis asked.

"She better not be," Garrett murmured in my ear as his arms tightened around my body. "I'll die before letting go of her."

His words warmed me, sending heat flaring through my body from the tips of my toes all the way to my cheeks.

Travis's mouth parted, and his white teeth shone in the moonlight filtering through the open curtains. Neither of them would allow the curtains to be closed since that first night when the soldiers had attacked. On the off-chance they returned, they wanted to see them coming. At least that's what they said, though I wondered sometimes if it was just so they could watch me sleep. Or they didn't like the dark. It was a toss-up.

"It's not that. I'm sad that my parents will not witness our vows, but I'm not doubting them at all."

"You still won't open to us completely, Charlie. I can feel the block on your magick. It flows between us, but not as completely as it should. You're holding back." Travis' words sliced through those bricks around my heart. Guilt was a powerful wrecking ball, but as fast as he tried to knock them down, I built them back up twice as thick.

"Why do you hold back, Charlotte? You are everything to us. We've pledged ourselves to you. To this pack. What more can we give you?" Garrett asked, his body flexing and stretching around mine as he fully woke from his brief nap, if five minutes could even be called a nap.

I lay in silence, wanting to tell them about the fear that plagued me, that paralyzed my mind. Instead I shook my head and attempted to lie. "I don't know. Everything is such a mess. I just need time."

"You can have the all the time you need, Charlie." Travis reached out and caught my chin, turning my face toward his. "But you can't lie. You used sex to avoid talking once already. And now you would choose to lie to my face?

Tears burned behind my eyelids as I squeezed them shut. I didn't want to lie. But I also didn't want to tell them I was purposefully holding back, refusing to allow the magick to settle completely. It was exhausting, but it was survival.

A second later, I was hanging over Garrett's legs, my belly pressed to his thighs and my ass straight up in the air. He moved so fast I didn't have time to protest before his palm connected with one of my butt cheeks.

"Ahhhhh!" I screeched, bucking against the heavy

forearm he had across my upper back to hold me down. Travis had jumped from the bed and was sitting on the floor, holding my arms, staring at me with eyes that reflected all my pain and guilt.

Another smack made me squirm. My ass stung, but it hurt my pride more than anything else.

"We are an alpha triad, but we are only as strong as our weakest link, Charlotte. If this continues, you will drag us down with your pack instead of giving us a fighting chance to save them," Garrett said, his voice deepening almost to a growl by the end. "Give it up, Charlotte. Let it go. Whatever eats at your heart and frightens you so much that you won't let your Fated mates anywhere near it."

"I can't!" I shouted, not caring a whit if the pack heard us or not. They didn't care about me. They hated me. Crawley had to stand outside our door when we slept. Thank the gods he'd come over to our side or Travis and Garrett would've insisted on taking shifts at the door. The curtains had to remain open at all times. "We aren't safe." The words slipped between another cry and a sob as Garrett's hand struck the curve of my panty-clad ass again. The lace was doing nothing to diffuse my mortification or the pain.

"You are safer with us than alone," Travis said from the floor in front of me. His hands squeezed my wrists gently as I tried to yank them free.

"Let me go. This is all I have left to give you. There's nothing else."

"You're still lying, Charlotte." Garrett's hand came down two more times, and tears ran down my cheeks.

"Our mate bond is strong, but it's not complete. That's on you. You have to let us in. You have to let it finish. We deserve to have all of you."

"No! If I let the bond completely settle, then I'll die when I lose you!" I cried, the words pouring out before I could stop them. *Damn them both. Sneaky bastards set me up.* "It will kill me. I can't lose more people. I have pack trying to assassinate me. A psychopath hunting me and mine. And now his soldiers are in town actively trying to take over the pack. My own uncle has turned against me and is bent on taking the whole pack down with him. You two are the only good thing I have left, but if I let myself l—" I cut myself off. I couldn't say it. But it didn't matter. They'd figured it out. I could see the pain reflected in the surface of Travis' irises. The tension melted from Garrett's body, and he let my body slip gently from his knees to the carpeted floor. Travis released my wrists and backed out of reach.

The distance from them both felt like a great chasm. The very thing I'd been trying to prevent had happened.

I'd lost them.

THE SUN ROSE, covering the fields behind the lodge with blankets of yellow and pink light. We stood holding hands, creating a small circle; the pack stood in a circle around us, also holding hands. Their circle represented the strength of the pack, uniting around the alphas. Our circle represented the heart and soul of the pack. Though the circles were complete and everyone held hands, there was no strength. No loyalty.

Even the magick between Garrett and Travis and I was weak, broken by the revelation in the bedroom only an hour before. The confession they'd coerced from my body by force had left our bond barely there. I couldn't understand why they remained. I'd all but told them I couldn't let myself love them.

Why did they stay at all? What was here for them? An angry pack and a mate who didn't deserve to be touched by them again. Yet they stood next to me, one on each side. Their hands gripped mine with strength and determination.

"As the sun rises and falls, as the moon rises and falls, also eternal will be my devotion to you. Fate has put us together, and nothing short of death will tear us apart." Travis spoke the words first, keeping my gaze locked with his. When he finished, his gaze moved to Garrett's and so did mine, locking onto the pain in Garrett's eyes.

What have I done? How can I throw this chance away because I am afraid? I wanted them so badly it hurt. They were all my heart longed for, but I wouldn't let my heart have them.

"As the sun rises and falls, as the moon rises and falls, also eternal will be my devotion to you. Fate has put us together, and nothing short of death will tear us apart." He spoke the same words, but unlike Travis' stony monotone voice, I could hear Garrett's pain. The pain of my lack of faith in them to win this fight. To keep us all safe. I was letting that psychopathic monster steal something from me, and he wasn't here. My fear was ruining my chance at happiness with these two men. My best friend, Eira, would've beaten me if she was here. She would've told me to *suck it up* and *take life by the horns* before it took me. She would live thousands of years longer than me, but she'd known love, and when her love had returned, she didn't let fear keep her from embracing her happiness.

"As the sun rises and falls... as the moon rises and falls... also eternal will be my devotion to both of you." I paused, looking to Travis and then again to Garrett. "Fate has put us together, and nothing short of death will tear us apart again." A tear ran down my cheek, but both my men smiled down at me. Magick surged through each of us, creating a circling ring that only death would break.

I let the love I'd been holding back pour out of me—a tsunami hurtling through me tearing down every brick of the wall I'd put up. My breath *whooshed* from my lungs, and I gasped for air as I felt their love fill my soul. The magick settled, and the waves calmed.

We were a triad.

We were alpha.

We were everything and more than I'd ever thought having a Fated mate would mean. Perhaps if I'd realized what it would feel like to join our souls, I wouldn't have pushed them away for so long. Maybe not at all.

CHAPTER
TWENTY-FOUR

GARRETT

I leaned against the wall behind Charlotte's chair in the great expanse of the lodge living area. The huge fireplace had been lit to roast a pig flank, and the scent of the barbecuing meat filled the room. Faces smiled that had been solemn during the ceremony as food and wine were enjoyed around the room in excess. We'd discreetly secured an unopened bottle of wine from the cellar and had only consumed it during the meal. Crawley had procured our food personally and tasted all of it before we ate.

Charlotte had finally accepted our bond, but that didn't mean she hadn't been right when she'd cried that we weren't safe. She was still afraid. I could smell it on her—an oily film that threatened to suffocate the happiness she'd taken the chance to reach for. And with good reason. Right now we were in a den that didn't belong to us.

Travis sat in the chair next to her. We took turns, though neither of us ever stopped watching her. After the second attempt on her life, it was difficult for us to let her use the bathroom without checking the window first and then standing guard outside the door.

Twice we'd almost lost her. At least Crawley added a third set of eyes. The young Lycan had proven himself a worthy beta. I just wished more of the pack would see through Victor's lies like he had. So far they smiled and moved about the room like nothing was amiss, but their eyes told another story entirely.

Lycans were unable to read each other's minds, but it was very difficult to hide everything. Our kind picked up on the smallest shifts in pheromones, pupil dilation, breathing, heart rate. Everything was noticed. Nothing was ignored.

Living in a pack was like being hooked up to a lie detector 24/7. It had its perks, like never having to wonder if your pack had your back, but it had its downsides, too. When disloyalty reared its head, it spread like a virus, infecting almost everyone.

Charlotte rose from her chair, and Travis stood immediately. "What can I get for you, sweetheart?"

"More wine?"

"I'll get another bottle."

"But there's more, just there," she said, pointing to the table. She turned slightly as she answered, the unspoken question of why we were only drinking from our own bottle hung between us, a ripcord waiting to be yanked. But it only took a few seconds for the answer to come to her. The rising pain in her gaze ripped a hole in my heart.

"Oh." The word floated in the air like a bubble waiting to be burst by the hatred simmering in the room. She sat down again, and Travis crossed the living area, maneuvering quickly through milling people and disappearing into the kitchen.

My chest tightened, and my heart froze momentarily. I knew my brother was more than capable of taking care of himself, but being alone meant vulnerability. I didn't think anyone would try to take him on, but Crawley noticed my discomfort immediately and nodded his head in the direction of the kitchen before following in my brother's footsteps.

Before he stepped out of view, Travis reappeared. Crawley was only a few feet away, and Travis raised a suspicious eyebrow at him before swinging his gaze across the room to me. He narrowed his gaze, but didn't give away whether he was annoyed or in agreement that we couldn't be too careful.

He used the corkscrew on the table in front of Charlotte to open the bottle then poured her a glass. She picked at her meal and tried to smile at a few people nearby. No one gave her a second look.

Movement in the entryway caught my eye. Victor ducked around the corner, and I heard the door open and close. I stepped forward from the wall and leaned down between Travis and Charlotte's heads. "Victor slipped out the front."

Travis nodded. "I think it's time we called in some help, Charlie. As long as your uncle is here and calling the shots behind the scenes, this will never be your pack. But the final choice is yours."

"I can't force them to accept us," Charlotte whispered.

"But you can force them to respect you," I said, laying a hand on her trembling shoulder. "We will let those leave who wish to follow Victor, but he must go, Charlotte. He can't be allowed to stay."

A sigh slipped from her chest, and her chin fell in defeat. "Do it."

Travis rose from his chair and disappeared from the room, shadowed by Crawley. I took his place in the chair next to Charlotte.

"You think they hate us now? Just wait until more of your people arrive and act like they are in charge," Charlotte warned.

"This is your ball game. We will fight for you, no matter what, but we can't fight everyone at once," I said, sliding my hand to the top of her bouncing thigh. "Breathe, my love."

"It's going to get worse before it gets better," she whispered.

I nodded. "Much."

CHAPTER
TWENTY-FIVE

TRAVIS

I went through the front door, stepped to the side, then sank onto one of the rockers facing the road in front of the lodge. Slipping the special cell phone I'd been given—courtesy of the Sanctuary witches, Meredith and Hannah—out of my pocket, I dialed the number at the top of my address book and waited as the phone rang.

"Hello?" Brogan's thick Irish accent rolled through the speaker. "What are you callin' me for? Didn't you marry that Mason woman today? Shouldn't you be in a bed somewhere making her scream for you? Or is yer brother doing it for you? Do you take turns?"

"Fuck off, asshole," I spit at the phone as a grin split my face. Leave it to Brogan to distract me from all the shit hovering above my head waiting to drop.

"I'm trying, but you called me, remember?" His laugh rolled through the speaker, and even Crawley was having a hard time not smiling. Brogan was a tough-as-nails sonofabitch and a giant among our kind, but he had a gift for raising spirits no matter the situation.

"Tell the girl she'll have to wait a minute."

"Who said it was just the one?" Brogan growled. A female giggled in the background of his phone call, and I shook my head. He really did have a woman with him.

"You know it's not noon yet," I said.

"Well, it's good I started early since you called and prolly want somethin' from me and the other guys. Rose said you were settling into a snake pit up there."

My eyes rolled. Of course Rose had known the second she stepped in the door. The woman claimed not to be psychic, but I assumed that, with thousands of years of history under her belt, she just knew. People hadn't changed much over the years, mostly just their wrapping.

"Have you heard from her lately? It's been a few days."

"Nope," Brogan answered. "But it's not like she'd call me personally. Still, Riley or the pixies would be talking about it if she had. The vampires never share anything, except that new one. Sweet little Bailey will crack like a ripe pecan if you ask nice enough."

"You better be careful. Erick is more than a little territorial. I'd hate to hear one of my favorite guys lost his arms to a Protector because he was cuddling up to a vampire's mate. I worked hard on those sleeves of yours. It would be such a waste."

Another bark of laughter cut through the quiet afternoon air. "Do you need me to come pull off some arms, Travis?"

"Maybe," I answered, shaking my head at Crawley's

wide-eyed speculation. "Mostly I just need more eyes and ears so they don't catch us unaware again. They've tried to kill her twice. And her uncle is working with an emissary from Xerxes. A squad attacked the lodge once already. The emissary claims they aren't with him, but that's a load of shit."

"How many do you need?"

"As many as you can stuff in that truck of yours," I answered.

Movement on the front lawn caught my attention. Victor was approaching on the sidewalk leading to the front door. Where he'd come from, I hadn't noticed.

"Get here quick, Brogan."

"Will do." The call ended with a beep.

Victor climbed the stairs, an ugly sneer spread across his face. "She was right not to trust you. You don't care about this pack. You're bringing your friends here to take over." He shoved past Crawley, knocking the slightly smaller man to the side and stomped through the front door.

Shit.

"Family, you've been waiting for them to show their true colors," Victor shouted into the living room full of eating people. "I just heard him calling in the cavalry. Their lackeys will be here shortly, and you can kiss the Mason pack goodbye as they shape it into what they want it to be. Charlie be damned as well. They won't respect her or us. How dare they bring in outsiders!"

Several shouts echoed his. Crawley and I shoved our way through the angry crowd to stand beside Garrett and Charlie.

"It's not what you think. He's lying to you," Charlie said, standing her ground.

"I just heard the phone call with my own ears," Victor said, snarling and snapping his teeth, showing his descended fangs. "He told him to bring as many as would fit in his truck. Or are you going to say I'm deaf, too?" The asshole held my gaze and grinned, flecks of yellow flashed in his irises.

"Two of this pack tried to murder Charlie. Kill her in cold blood. If it was your mate who'd almost died in front of you twice, wouldn't you do anything to protect them?" I raised my voice just slightly; the power that came with being alpha hit them like an ax to a tree.

The mumblings and growls were silenced, and even Victor was having trouble mouthing back after my show of authority. He may want to be alpha and have most of the pack following his lead, but he was *not* their alpha yet. The magick bonding the pack together hadn't abandoned the three of us. I could feel it coursing strongly through me.

I hated them for being disloyal and working against my brother and mate, I would fight and give my life to protect them and make sure they had the best chance at survival. Such was the mantle of pack alpha. Garrett and Charlie would feel the same, but as the oldest male in our triad, I wore the heaviest burden of responsibility as well as the strongest ability to wield our power.

"Fate matched us with your alpha female. We knew she was meant to be ours from the first moment we laid eyes on her. You test the will of the goddesses with your disloyalty. And because this pack is broken, I have called in help to manage the problem. Two attempts on the life of mine and my brother's mate are two too many. Until this pack gets its shit together or comes apart completely, I will do everything in my power to protect what is mine."

Charlie slipped her hand into mine. "He asked and I gave permission. You are my family. But I can't trust you. I don't deserve this, and neither do my mates. This behavior will not stand, and my parents would be ashamed if they could see what you've become. What you've let Victor turn you into."

"You led our family to their deaths!" shouted a voice from across the room.

Before she could answer, I thundered a reply, shaking the room with my anger. How dare they blame her for something out of her control? "You think she would willingly lead her family to their deaths? She watched Xerxes cut her parents to pieces in front of her. The only reason she is alive today is because the woman who betrayed her in the first place had a change of heart and helped her escape with the few people Xerxes hadn't had time to kill yet."

"You think Victor has your best interests at heart? He's trying to get you to surrender to the very person who stole everything from you. Why can't you see that?" Garrett added.

Victor scoffed and stepped forward. "It's all words. You don't know what really happened, and I have the emissary's word that Xerxes wants all of us to live. We just have to stop fighting him. He's not the enemy the Masons made him out to be. All these years he's been trying to find a way to give us the upper hand over the humans.

Aren't you tired of being a second-class citizen in their eyes? It's time they recognized us for the powerful race we are and respected us for it."

Fists lifted around the room. He'd won them over again. It would never stop. He would never stop. Until the pack was all dead. Or Victor was. Hopefully Brogan and some of the other guys from Sanctuary would show up before a mini war started tearing this place apart.

"Get out!" Charlie raised her voice, using some of our alpha magick to get the point across to Victor. The room vibrated with our power, and voices quieted instantly. "You have finally worn down all of my patience, Uncle Victor. Since the formal challenge and fight wasn't enough to satisfy your hatred of me, I will leave. If you want Victor, you can have him. Leave me and mine in peace while we pack."

No one spoke another word or moved, except Victor, who backed away slowly and then slammed the door behind him as he went. No one followed him. The ones who'd rallied behind him moments ago–gone.

I glanced over at my brother and he nodded, following my gaze to the back door Victor had exited through. We both wanted to know where he was going and who he was meeting.

CHAPTER
TWENTY-SIX

CHARLIE

I stared down at the rug on my bedroom floor. I couldn't believe I'd just told my pack I'd leave. Every bone in my body screamed out it was wrong. I couldn't abandon them to the fate Xerxes would dole out. Either he'd kill them all slowly or kill them quickly. The outcome would be the same.

Death.

As alpha, they were my responsibility. Hell, they'd been my responsibility, along with my parents', for years. I'd been groomed to take over in case my parents were captured and killed. But when it'd actually happened, though we'd talked about it, I wasn't ready. I wasn't prepared to see them tortured and humiliated and brutally murdered in front of me.

Sometimes I could hear my mother's screams as he gutted her and my father's pleas before the animal slit her throat. It had been pleasurable to him. He'd enjoyed killing for killing's sake. Their pain, their screams. It was sick, but that's what he seemed to like the most.

I'd heard the term psychopath tossed around from time to time in conversation, but he was the only one I'd ever seen in real life. Witnessed the pain he spread. I could hear his dark voice slithering through my soul, tendrils of evil waiting to snuff out any light they could find.

A hand fell on my shoulder, and I screeched, nearly jumping out of my skin.

"It's just me, love," Garrett said, keeping his voice low and soft. I turned into him and buried my face in his chest. Inhaling his scent, I released the breath I'd been holding since he startled me. That triggered an epic meltdown. Tears poured from my eyes, and my knees sagged.

Travis approached my back and leaned forward, pinning me between them. A safe sandwich of sexy Lycan that smelled good enough to lick from head to toe.

Here I was crying my eyes out, worried about the end of the pack and lodge I'd called home for eighty years, and my mind drifted to sex. What was wrong with me?

Even if I didn't get sex, I just wanted them to hold me. Wrapping my arms around Garrett's neck, I pulled myself up his body. He met me halfway, and our lips collided. My tongue danced with his, fighting to taste every inch of his mouth. His did the same, making long sweeps between my lips and pulling my lips, one at a time, into his mouth.

My panties were wet, and I moaned, rubbing against the hard-on Garrett had pressed tightly against my belly.

Travis' hard cock nestled against my ass, and I couldn't help but rock back and forth between them, enjoying the pressure from both sides.

"You're not going to be mad at me this time, are you?" I whispered against Garrett's mouth before turning my head to meet Travis' lips where they'd been nibbling on my earlobe.

"No, sweetheart. Tonight is about new beginnings and embracing the choices and commitments we all made publicly today."

"I especially liked the choice you made to allow our bond to settle. I can't tell you how happy that makes me, Charlotte," Garrett murmured into my ear as I kissed Travis over my shoulder.

Their hands were everywhere. My breasts. My hips. Inside my pants. Then fingers were inside me, coaxing out an orgasm that no doubt would be one of many tonight.

I shuddered and gasped, letting the mini-quake spread from my belly outward until my fingers dug into Garrett's neck and my toes curled in the fibers of the carpet.

Travis dragged his body down my back, catching the hem of my pants with his fingers and pulled until they dropped to the floor along with my panties in a pool of fabric around my bare feet. Then his mouth kissed up the back side of one thigh and down the other.

I was shaking by the time he finished.

Garrett had skillfully relieved me of my shirt and bra, so I stood naked between them... while they were still fully dressed. Totally not fair.

Yanking at Garrett's shirt, I tried to pull it up a little, but he pushed away my hand and lowered his mouth to one of my bare breasts. His tongue swirled around the nipple until it turned to steel. Then he did the same to the other breast. Both throbbed from the attention, and I moaned when his mouth moved lower, trailing down my torso toward my slick pussy. All thoughts of his shirt vanished.

I wanted his mouth on me. And Travis. Where was Travis? The heat from his body was gone from my back, but I saw him a few seconds later, emerging from the bathroom with something black in his hands. I couldn't quite make out the item before he hid it behind his back with a mischievous smile.

Garrett's mouth reached my slit, and I nearly fell on top of him. His arms slipped beneath my thighs and gripped my hips, lifting and moving us to the bed. For a second, his mouth left me, and I moaned again, needing to feel his tongue against my clit and thrusting inside me until he was ready to thrust that hard cock of his inside instead.

Travis caressed my breasts again, one at a time, bringing each nipple to a hard peak for a second time. Then he slipped the black thing I'd seen him with—a scarf of mine—over my eyes and tied it gently around my head. Losing sight of them made me focus even harder on my sense of touch, smell, and every sound they made.

"Please," I moaned. My body burned for both of them.

"Yes, love," Travis said, his voice softer than I'd heard it all day. He rolled me to my side, facing me away from him and lifted my leg. He rubbed his fingers, covered in a cooling gel, along my slit and up between the cheeks of my ass, being especially careful to spread the lubricant around the tight rosebud of muscles he wanted to fuck. At least I hoped that was his plan.

Garrett's scent drifted to my nostrils, and the bed dipped as he lay down in front of me. My hands flew to his now naked chest, and a shiver of delight ran down my body. I slid my hand lower and lower, following the lines of his body, stopping to pause at the giant erection meant just for me.

Gods, I wanted him. Wrapping my fingers around his hard shaft, I pulled gently, drawing the tip of his cock back and forth across my trembling belly. He groaned, his chest vibrating with a carnal growl that made my pussy weep.

"Now," I demanded, a little more forcefully.

Garrett hooked a heel around my leg, and his arm snaked around my waist. A second later, he rolled me into position on top of him and had moved us down the bed closer to the edge. My knees on either side of him were still on the mattress, but my feet were hanging off into the air.

I lifted my body, felt for his cock, and guided it to my pussy, sinking down and taking him in with one thrust. His hands locked around my hips and held me for a few seconds before letting me rock against him.

My vision was gone, but I could hear both their hearts pounding. Travis placed a hand on my back and pushed until I was lying flat against Garrett's chest.

More gel cooled between the cheeks of my ass, and

then the tip of his cock pressed ever so gently at first. He put a foot up on the bed next to my thigh and pressed again, this time entering and sending me spiraling into oblivion as another orgasm rocked my body.

"That's it, love," Travis said, sliding even deeper.

Garrett thrust in and out slowly as Travis continued to push deeper. My body flexed and trembled. The orgasm had faded, but another was already curling in my belly as both my mates filled me completely.

I liked the blindfold. It let me focus completely on every touch, kiss, and thrust. They slowly increased their speed, and I moaned, pleasure filling me with bliss as it washed away my worry and frustrations. The problems with the pack disappeared, and I was able to just *be* with my mates. Problems would always need to be solved, but this bond we had with each other would never fade.

They were with me, and I was with them—a triad alpha group, but now three joined souls.

I bit into Garrett's shoulder and screamed as yet another orgasm slammed through me; were it not for them holding me up, I would've collapsed into a boneless mound. Both men groaned as well, following my climax with their own.

Travis pulled away first and, from the sound of his footsteps, headed for my bathroom. Garrett lifted me by my hips, and I moaned. Every muscle in my body was tired and content at the same time. Moving was not necessary, yet he continued to lift my body, setting me gently in the center of the bed. He tugged the blindfold free from my head, and I smiled, meeting his contented gaze.

Travis returned, and they cleaned me and then themselves before climbing back into bed with me and snuggling on both sides. They had my back—and my front. But mostly, I knew for sure they would support me no matter what.

CHAPTER
TWENTY-SEVEN

CHARLIE

We made love several more times that evening, slowly then fiercely then slowly again. When the sun rose that morning and peeked through the curtains on my window, I could honestly say I only wanted to snuggle closer to the two men on either side of me and pretend morning hadn't arrived.

But we were all awake. I heard the shift in both their heart rates only seconds after I opened my eyes.

"We could just stay here. In bed."

"We could," Garrett said, his voice as soft as crushed velvet.

"But?" I asked. There would be a "but." I could hear it coming.

"We need to get out and look for those soldiers. They could return at any time. No matter what the pack votes about us, we need to be prepared." Travis ran his fingertips along the curve of my bare hip, making my body twitch when he hit a ticklish nerve.

"I don't want you to leave without me."

"No," Travis growled.

"Let me phrase this a different way. You aren't leaving me here while you two go gallivanting around town looking for a small army of heavily-armed Lycans bent on killing you." I sat up between them and crossed my arms. "So either you take me with you or you don't go at all."

"You're not a trained soldier, Charlie. Just let us do a little recon, and we'll be back before everyone has eaten their breakfast."

I snorted; Travis' words were a pile of dog shit, and he knew it. "Look who's lying now. Just try and leave without me, pal." I glared down at him, and he frowned.

"We won't leave you." He finally caved, but it was short-lived. "But when Brogan and the others arrive, you stay. No questions or complaints."

I opened my mouth to argue, but Garrett's mouth caressed my bare shoulder, and I moaned something unintelligible instead.

"Promise, Charlotte," he whispered.

"I promise," I said, rolling my head to the side, giving him more access to my shoulder and neck.

"We could also just stay up here and continue to play hide-the-cock." I smiled, lying down between them and spreading my legs as far open as their closeness would allow.

"Cheater," Garrett said first, moving his hand to my slick folds and burying two fingers inside. "So wet. It would be a shame, brother, not to make sure our new mate wasn't completely satisfied before we leave her alone for several hours."

A smile spread across my face, and I moaned as Garrett's touch fanned the flame of desire already burning brightly inside me.

His next few moves flipped me to my stomach. Then he pulled my ass into the air until I was up on all fours. I gasped as his cock thrust hard, seating himself inside me with one movement.

Travis had other ideas in mind and nudged the tip of his cock against my lips.

I opened and sucked him inside, rolling my tongue around the head and then beneath, lubricating the shaft.

His hands slid into my hair and took a firm grip. "Open more, Charlie," he murmured.

I relaxed my jaw and allowed myself to give them complete control. Soon they had synced their rhythm, pulling in and out against each other. When Garrett filled my pussy, Travis pulled out of my mouth and then vice versa. Slow and steady, until my body was shaking, arms and legs threatening to collapse once again.

Garrett stiffened behind me and thrust deep. His warm cum filled me, and I cried out around Travis' cock as my body joined in his ecstasy. Travis reached his climax only moments later, and I swallowed his seed as it shot down the back of my throat.

Once they stepped away, I dropped flat on the mattress and closed my eyes. There was nothing I wanted more than to sleep another few hours. Garrett left the bed and returned shortly with a warm washrag and cleaned my face and then between my legs.

"You rest, Charlotte."

"I'm going with you," I murmured, snuggling into one of the soft pillows near the headboard.

"To the shower?" he asked, sarcasm coloring his voice.

"You can do that by yourself." I opened one eye and spied Travis sitting in the recliner across the room. He'd found boxers to put on and winked when he caught my gaze.

"Sleep, love."

I nodded my head and closed my eyes again, shocked they were giving me what I wanted. Maybe they had changed their minds and were going to stay in my room with me all day.

They're gone!

I sat up abruptly, and the covers slid down my still-naked body. The fucking bastards had lied. Tricked me with amazing sex, showered, and snuck out.

In ten seconds flat, I'd found clothes and yanked them on, but when I tried the doorknob, it didn't turn. I shook it harder and then kicked at the base of the door.

Taking a deep breath, I scented Crawley in the hallway. His heartbeat was sporadic, and his breathing shallow. "Let me out, Crawley."

"I can't."

"I'll take down this door!" I slammed my palm against it. "Open it!"

"They ordered me not to let you leave. They said to tell you they would be back before the sun set."

"I am your alpha! Open this door."

"I can't. They said you would argue and insist on going after them, but that you were pregnant."

Pregnant. The word hit my belly like a rock. I wasn't. *Was I?* I would know. My finger flew to my mouth, and I nicked the tip with a canine. The metallic taste of blood filtered into my mouth, but my hormone levels were normal. There was no pregnancy. *Fucking liars!*

"I'm not! You can taste my blood. I'm not. Open this door."

"No, Charlie. Whether you are or you aren't, you know very well that if I open this door I'd have to restrain you, and I don't want to do that."

Fine. I backed away slowly and walked toward the large picture window in my room that faced the front driveway of the lodge. If I couldn't go out the door, then I'd just have to go out a window.

I shook my head. How dare they make up some story about me being pregnant to get Crawley to keep me locked away? I grabbed a pair of combat boots from against the wall and jammed my feet inside them. Walking to my vanity, I reached beneath the table part in the center and pulled a handgun from the holster taped underneath. After tucking it in the waistband of my jeans, I slowly unlatched the window and raised it in the frame. Eventually he would realize I was gone, but not before it was too late to catch me.

If those Lycan turncoats hadn't beaten the shit out of Travis and Garrett, I would.

I lowered myself from the roof and leapt to the ground, crouching low to absorb the jarring impact. No one shouted. None of the doors on the lodge opened.

A few minutes later, I was jogging down the road. If I took a vehicle, I'd never be able to scent and follow the two jerks. When I reached the massive bur oak tree an easy quarter mile from the lodge, I ducked under the low-hanging branches and stripped down, folding and tucking my shoes and clothes into the waiting empty wooden boxes nailed along the top of one of the lowest branches. This tree had been used for generations by my pack as a glorified locker room.

I stretched my arms over my head and rolled my neck from side to side. My magick rippled and tickled my skin, prickling as I drew the change forward. A few seconds later, I dropped to all fours.

My wolf came forward, and the hunt was on.

CHAPTER
TWENTY-EIGHT

XERXES

"Give me one." I rolled my neck and growled at the slow human who held the key to me taking more power from the humans. The ability to hide in plain sight, such an underplayed characteristic of the Kitsune. They didn't use their ability to their advantage and look what it got them. They were nearly extinct. Well, at least that's what they claimed.

I chuckled. They could be hiding in plain sight for all I knew. Just because the ones in Tokyo lived in a commune separate from the rest of humanity didn't mean all of their kind were solitary hermits. Although, after I burned that commune to the ground and took Riza and Sochi, it was quite possible that they were the only two living adult Kitsune in this dimension.

Unfortunately for them, I knew what they looked like and where they would both be living. Not that I really wanted to take on four angry Drakonae and a bitchy

Lamassu who thought I stabbed her husband in the back. Still... knowing where the Kitsune would be could be helpful one day in the future, especially since Sochi's first daughter remained in my possession. With enough patience, I wouldn't need her mother or her aunt again. In a couple decades, she could safely produce several babies a year. More than enough to provide me with all the infant blood I could possibly need to dose any and every supernatural willing to work for me.

And there were hundreds so far. The last report I'd gotten from Manda said my army numbered about eight hundred strong. She'd recalled the alphas, generals, and chiefs of the clans who led those loyal to me. They would receive the dose first. Then what had been left was dispersed to them to use on the men they deemed worthiest first. The men most loyal to them and to our cause.

The lab coat handed me a syringe filled with a pink liquid. So easy. Just one shot and *poof,* technology couldn't tell us from any other human. I took it and jammed it into my upper arm, pushing the liquid slowly into my body. A strange tingling started in my arm and traveled down my side, my legs, then up my other side, into my other arm until I could feel it everywhere. Every cell throbbed with the mix of magick and science inside those little molecules. I closed my eyes for a second, and the hum from the serum faded away.

I was myself again. No tingle. No hum. I'd been informed this was perfectly normal for all subjects.

"Scan me."

"Sir?"

The lab coat started toward me, but didn't make eye contact. Almost as if...

It couldn't be. I walked to the glass door behind me. My heart raced. There was no reflection. I was standing in front of the glass, invisible. A second later, I appeared again. Fully there, no transparency.

"Sir!" The lab coat squeaked in surprise.

I whirled, growling. This was a complication that could be useful, but not if I couldn't control it. "Scan me." If the Kitsune blood affected me differently than the other subjects, I could only hope that it would at least hide me from the scans.

He held up the piece of black technology with a round lens in the middle. It looked like a portable iris scanner.

I leaned down and let it scan my eye.

"Positive for human, sir." He flipped the device around so I could see the green flashing screen.

A smile spread across my face. "Good. Now I just need to learn how to control the camouflage aspect of my new ability."

The man gulped and nodded, backing away slowly.

"How many more doses do you have?"

"Ms. Farrok has scheduled three dozen more for today, and we are sending the remaining doses with them as you requested. They will disperse to their men when they return home."

"Good. You've done well..." I glanced at his coat tag. "Henry. I'll make sure Manda sends a gift to your family. I'm sure they'll be proud to hear how you are serving your country so bravely."

The trembling bug of a man in front of me nodded and continued to back away. I snorted and left the lab. Everything was going as planned for once, everything except the Djinn female, who had been overshadowing every move I made over the last couple of days. Ever since she escaped her death.

Still, she was a clever woman, never staying for more than a few seconds. If it hadn't been for the mirrors in my office, I wouldn't have realized she'd returned to the mansion and was following me. But a few sightings of her reflection made me hyperaware. Now I noticed her in hallway shadows, disappearing behind corners, and once in my bedroom. She was being extremely cautious, though not cautious enough. She knew who and what I was, and I her.

After getting a good look at her in the reflection of a mirror in my bedroom, there was no mistaking her identity. Manda's mother, Asa Jelveh Hamideh-Farrok, was not a woman who would abandon her daughter. Eventually, she would make a mistake, and I would carry out her execution.

It was only a matter of time. And I had plenty.

All the soldiers in the house knew to watch for her. The last thing I needed was her communicating with Manda. I put several newly inoculated Lycans on her detail along with two Djinn as transporters. Her mother wouldn't be getting anywhere near her daughter, and if any of the Djinn reacted the way the last messenger did, the Lycans were under orders to kill them.

I climbed the stairs to the upper level of the mansion and grimaced as the baby's crying pierced the usually quiet house. She rarely cried, but ever since Sochi had been stolen away, it was like the little wretch knew. The doctors had cleared her after the latest blood draw. She needed three weeks between them to fully recover, meaning the next one would be her last. After another rest period, she would be too old. Her blood would no longer be viable in the serum.

Turning on the stairs, I changed my mind and returned to the bottom. A messenger blinked into the foyer ahead of me and bowed.

"Sir."

"What is it?"

"Max reported back that the Mason pack is dividing. Most appear to be following Victor, but the new alphas are not. Charlie, the Mason daughter, and her mates are packing to leave Ada. The pack takes a vote in two days on whether or not she stays."

Fucking idiots. "I told him I wanted the alpha female. If she isn't coming, then I want her dead. Is that clear? They can all die if I can't have her."

"Yes, sir," the Djinn answered, bowing again and teleporting from the room.

Manda's familiar scent drifted to me from across the room. "I'm going to kill your friend. Either her pack will offer her up on a silver platter or my soldiers will murder her in her bed." I turned to the right and narrowed my gaze. She stood stiff and straight. Her black business suit sagged on her thinning frame, and her cheeks were hollower than they'd been a few weeks ago. "If you don't eat and take care of yourself, I'll have to make it someone's personal mission to make sure you do by *any* means of coercion necessary. I'm sure either of your bodyguards would find the offer quite attractive," I said, nodding to the two Lycans standing just behind her.

She swallowed and nodded. "I'll be sure to take more time to eat, sir."

"Good. Then I expect you won't look like a worn out dishrag the next time I see you. The SECR Director of Defense should not ever look like a starving wretch. Is that clear?"

"Yes, sir," she answered again, with more gusto this time.

"I'm looking forward to you watching me kill your friend. It will be the highlight of my week, for sure. Although the invasion of the Washington Republic will be hard to beat."

CHAPTER
TWENTY-NINE

TRAVIS

"She's not going to trust us again after this," Garrett growled.

I shook my head, watching the warehouse where we'd tracked a werewolf to earlier in the day. The soldier had gone in, but it'd been an hour, and nothing. We'd been sitting in Crawley's truck, as far from the building as possible, but close enough to watch the door.

"Bringing her wasn't an option. I refuse to put her in *more* unnecessary danger. It's bad enough leaving her at the lodge."

"So putting our entire mate bond, not to mention our balls, in danger was the better option. She's a fighter, Travis. Don't you remember how—"

My brother was too quick to forget. "Don't you remember what she looked like when we pulled her out of Savannah with the others?" I snarled, keeping my voice low, but my anger stirred the beast inside me, and I knew my eyes had lit for a few seconds.

"That's not fair. She'd been captured, injured, and had just watched her parents die. She didn't deserve the way we just... snuck out. Like cowards."

The comment was a jab, and it worked. Leaving her felt wrong from my head to my heart, but every time I thought of Charlie fighting, I remembered seeing her limping down the street in Savannah—bruised, bloody, and broken. The thought of seeing her like that again burned in my gut like fire.

I'd seen death. Torture. Chaos. I'd seen things happen in this world as the United States had fallen apart that should've broken me, but it hadn't. Not only that, I'd found peace in a tattoo parlor surrounded by other supernaturals I was supposed to avoid and/or hate. Then Garrett had shown up, too.

But peace was short-lived, and the next fight was always only a stone's throw away. Our next fight was coming soon. Whatever was necessary to protect Charlie, that was the mission. Rose told us before we left –*protect your mate.*

Garrett told me about working with the military of the West Coast Republic, but when they'd realized he was a Lycan, it'd been all he could manage just to get out alive. After that, he wandered from one city to another, never settling in one place for long. It was hard to get to Texas if you didn't know a good way across the border. I'd been lucky. I found my way to Texas early and, like Killían, had been recruited, working special ops for the

TR for years. Eventually, I'd just gotten tired of the blood and left. Word of mouth had led me to Sanctuary.

Rose had offered me a place. And I opened the tattoo shop shortly after, a skill I'd learned from my father years ago. Travis and I both had always loved the art our father brought to life on people's bodies. We were both good artists and had a gift with needle and ink.

Garrett leaned forward in the truck, his eyes glued to the door across the street as if it'd come to life and waved at him.

"What?" I whispered, focusing my vision and hearing.

"There are more arriving," he answered. "Two... no, three more heartbeats just came in from the other side of the building."

I could hear them, too. The traffic passing us on the road made it difficult to pick out their voices, but if they were coming and going through the front door, that's where we should be.

"Let's circle around to the front and see what they have to offer."

Garrett nodded.

A few turns later, I stopped the truck across the street from the warehouse in question. I knew it was the same. The green tin roof was unique in its line up, but the sign on the front disturbed me more than it should've. *Ada Soup Kitchen.*

"Fuck me." Air whooshed from Garrett's lungs, and I growled in frustration.

"Are we sure the dude we followed was one of them?" I asked.

"Yes," Garrett nodded again. "I know it was him. I remember his scent distinctly."

"Fine. Then we go in and have a look around."

"No."

It was risky. Too many civilians. If they opened fire, people could get hurt. Garrett and I might heal faster, but getting shot still hurt like a bitch and could kill us if they hit the right spot—our heart. We could regenerate fast, but a bullet in the heart just wasn't something our bodies could repair before too much blood was lost.

"Fine." I turned my attention to the building again.

My body reacted before my mind processed. Her scent filled my lungs, and I swung open the driver's side door.

"Charlie!" I shouted, sprinting for the front door where several people were staring at the beautiful silver wolf. But it was the men in black coming through the front door who worried me the most.

Garrett was instantly beside me. The wolf hesitated her next step and turned to look at me. I waved my arm to the side. "Run!"

The soldiers saw us, too, and then they saw her. Before she could move an inch, half a dozen furry red darts hit her chest, and she yelped before shuddering and falling to the concrete.

People were yelling and scattering every which direction, but Garrett and I just kept running toward her.

The soldiers were close, too, but I'd die before letting them take her from me. What in the gods was she doing out here anyway? Crawley would be getting more than an earful when I got back.

They shot a few times at us, but knowing they were coming and being on the move made them easy to duck to one side or the other to avoid the darts. We reached Charlie's body first, and I scooped her up off the road and ducked down through an alley that led around the large building. Garrett rotated his body and hauled butt back to the car.

He'd seen me take the alley, and I knew he'd be waiting on the next street over. Boots pounded behind me, but I stayed focused on listening for the whir of air preceding a dart. Two more narrowly missed my shoulder before Garrett squealed the truck to a stop right in front of me. I yanked open the backseat door, tossed Charlie more roughly than I intended, and climbed into the front, closing the door behind me just as another volley of darts pinged the closed windshield and metal of the door.

"Go!"

He pressed his foot to the floor, and we left.

Nothing had been accomplished. We didn't know the plans the soldiers had for the Mason pack. But we did now know that Charlie was more pissed than we'd first estimated. Not only had she followed us, against our orders, the woman had tracked us across fifteen miles of city. Managing that when your prey was in a vehicle was impressive.

She loved her pack, but she'd lost everything. It'd been unfair to think she wouldn't go postal when she realized we left her. We'd told her we were a team, but when we'd been tested, we'd failed her. Though she hadn't really been alone—Crawley had been outside her door—it was still a betrayal, one that would cost us dearly. I was just grateful we'd been able to grab her before they did.

"You fucking bastard!" The words hit hard, but not like her heel to my stomach.

Air *uuumphed* from my lungs, and I gasped to refill.

"Both of you!"

I took in the beautiful vision of her lovely naked body, and she withdrew immediately, curling into the opposite corner of the truck like a crab hiding in its shell. She wrapped her arms around her knees and hugged her legs against her chest. Her scent soothed my wolf. We'd both been worried our error in judgment had cost us our mate.

"I'm sorry." The words were bitter in my mouth, but the truth. She deserved the truth.

"Sorry doesn't cut it. You lied. The pack is falling apart because Victor is lying to them about the fate Xerxes promised. And you *lie* to me. After you told me you wouldn't leave, you did! What kind of fucking asshole does that? I deserve better."

Her eyes glittered with anger. Not hatred, thank the gods. But she was spitting mad and well within her rights to be so.

"I'm sorry, Charlotte," Garrett echoed from the driver's seat. "We were trying to pro—"

"Save it," she spat out. "Just drive. When you get to the big oak tree on the long driveway, stop and let me out."

My eyebrows scrunched together. "Why?"

"My clothes are in the tree, genius. Anything else I need to explain, past the fact that I'm perfectly capable of taking care of myself and going on missions? If you had just let me go with you this morning, none of this would've happened."

"We know," Garrett and I said at the same time.

"I'm really pissed at you. At both of you."

Neither of us spoke again. We both knew she was right. A part of me wanted to beg for her forgiveness, but the hard part of my heart justified my actions and wouldn't let me.

My cell phone buzzed in my pocket, and I pulled it out, surprised to see Rose's name blinking on the face.

"Rose?" I said, swiping the answer box.

"Travis. We are on our way back with Sochi."

"So you got her out. That's good. Is she okay?"

"Physically, she appears in good health. She is pregnant, and Riza said she was only sixteen, so that worries me. But both their heartbeats are steady and strong. She's in some type of induced coma. Whatever he had her on is taking a long time to leave her system."

"She's still out?" I asked.

"Yes. We plan to drive non-stop. We need to cross the border quickly so Killían already called ahead to his old contacts. They let the platoon at Vicksburg Bridge know to expect us. We'll cross there later tonight and, hopefully, be in Ada by late tomorrow afternoon."

"Good. No one got hurt?"

"Everything worked as planned. For once, he wasn't a step ahead of the game. He realized mid-way through the meet, but by then it was too late," Rose continued.

I chuckled. "I guess that means Calliope hasn't lost her charm in her old age."

"I heard that, asshole." Calliope's voice hollered out

from a few feet away from Rose's phone. "Do I need to show you my charm when you get home?"

I didn't reply. *Home* was with Charlie. Not in Sanctuary. Only if the pack she'd loved and protected for nearly a century kicked her to the curb would Sanctuary ever be my home again. I hadn't realized how attached I'd gotten to everyone. My chest tightened, and I took a slow breath.

"How is your mate, Travis?"

"Things are chaotic here, Rose. There's an emissary from Xerxes trying to convince the pack to pick up and join his side. Waving a fucking white flag one second and trying to murder the three of us in our sleep the next."

"How are you, Travis?" the Sentinel asked, pressing deeper.

"I'm glad you'll be here tomorrow, Rose." I would be. The Sentinel of Sanctuary was a mother figure to most in the town. She might not always act all lovey-dovey, but she was the glue that held everything together. She was the heart and soul of the place, and without her, it would collapse into chaos. With her, it was a beautiful hub of loyalty and friendship.

"We'll see you then. Tell her you love her." The line went dead before I could comment on her last words. She always knew. That was Rose. Somehow, the universe just made sure she knew how everything was going. Though she asked how things were, it was just her way of being polite. More than likely, she already knew the answer. Something about living in town with her made a person connected to her.

I shoved the phone back into my pocket and caught Charlie's gaze.

"Why would she tell you that?"

Of course she'd heard. Lycans could eavesdrop from a half mile away. She was barely two feet from me.

"Because it's the truth, Charlotte," Garrett said before I could. "We love you more than anything in this world. Finding you was Fate's way of giving us another chance to have a fulfilling life. When our family died, we lost everything. Even our hope."

"You lied."

"Travis won't admit it, but we were scared to bring you with us. You've been so emotionally volatile. Two of your own tried to kill you. Your uncle is still trying to steal the pack from under your nose. And Xerxes has Lycans out on the warpath for your blood, and we just couldn't... we just couldn't drag you out into this. We needed to know exactly what we were up against and—"

"And we are used to doing everything ourselves," I finished.

She turned her head away from me and stared out the window. "Pull over here." Her words were flat. Her pulse was steady. I wanted more than anything to know what she was thinking, but she was masking it.

Garrett put the truck in park, and she opened the door. Her hips rocked with each step, showing off her round ass as she walked away. A second later, she'd ducked beneath the branches and was completely hidden from view.

"This can't happen again, Travis."

I nodded. He'd been against leaving her at the beginning, but I'd convinced him otherwise. The blame sat squarely on my shoulders, and I could feel its weight bearing down.

A few moments later, she appeared in a pair of jeans, a t-shirt, and a flopping pair of unlaced combat boots. When she slid into the back seat again, I saw the bulge of a handgun on her back. I peered through the window past her, trying to see through the leaves and branches. *A locker room.* It was where they left clothes when they shifted. *Very convenient.*

Garrett started forward again, and within a couple of minutes, we could see the front of the lodge. A large black SUV was parked, and several men were leaning against the back and side of it.

"The guys are here," Garrett said.

CHAPTER
THIRTY

CHARLIE

"Of course your friends arrive while we're gone. I'm sure Victor is having a great ol' time riling everyone up over this."

"Charlotte," Garrett growled. "We need the help."

"I know," I mumbled, staring at the hodgepodge of guys hovering around the big black SUV. I recognized a couple of them from my visits into Sanctuary, but couldn't remember any names.

Our truck stopped, and I climbed out behind Garrett. Travis walked around the opposite way and greeted the men. Two were similar in size and looks, blonde, green eyes, and smiles that probably melted panties right off of women, although the one on the left was a little bigger and tougher looking than his counterpart. Both were taller than my mates, but not by much.

"Brogan." Travis shook the giant's hand on the left.

"Have you met Charlie before?" He gestured to me, and I nodded, stepping forward.

"Seen in passing," the big man answered, "but not officially met. It's lovely to meet the woman who kept these two simpering like puppies left out in the cold. It was good for them to wait. Made the gett'n all that much better."

I couldn't help the smile that crept across my face. Pissed at my mates or not, I liked this guy.

"This is my cousin, Liam. Don't let his good looks fool you; he's a devil if there ever was one."

"It's nice to put a face with the name, Charlie." The second blonde giant extended his hand, and I shook it before turning to the other two men standing to the side.

They were both average size for a Lycan, which meant six-foot-five or so. But one had blazing red hair and blue eyes, while the other was wearing two days' worth of black scruff and had curls that I'm sure women wanted to sink their fingers into. His brown eyes were dark and cold, like he'd seen more than his fair share of pain over the years. I wondered how old he was. Streaks of gray hair were scattered around his temples.

"Maddock," the red head said, stepping forward. He nodded his head, but didn't extend his hand. "My cohort is Douglas. He's not much of a talker, but he'll chew ass like a hungry lion in an arena."

My eyes widened at the imagery. Maybe he could chew off Victor's ass. "Thank you for coming, but why are you standing in the parking lot?"

"Your people weren't that keen on letting us in," Brogan answered.

"Where's Finn?" Travis asked.

"Finn's mate is in labor," Liam said, stepping closer to the group. His deep voice was gravely and made the hair on the back of my neck stand on end.

"We're missing Teagan's baby?" Garrett asked.

"She'll probably already have it before we sort out your mess here and get back," Liam answered.

"Who do we have to kill to get the ball rolling?" Douglas stepped forward.

My hand flew to my mouth, and I whirled to face Travis. *What the fuck?* I mouthed, narrowing my gaze.

"Douglas, we don't—"

The big dark-haired man smirked. "It were just a thought.

"Killing isn't always necessary in all situations, Douglas," Maddock growled.

"If so, I'm calling it," Douglas said, his mouth curving into a wickedly frightening smile.

His Scottish accent distracted me slightly from the fact that he wanted to know whose head was on the chopping block.

"I'll tell you what," I said. "If that fucking emissary from Xerxes shows his face at this lodge again, you can kill him."

The big man cracked his knuckles and nodded. "Verra good."

"So are we going to go in or just stand out here jawing?" Brogan asked, gesturing to the front door with a wave of his hand.

"Come on," Travis said, as we all moved toward the front door together.

"Who's the punk watching us from the trees?"

I whirled in time to see a flash of black disappear for a moment before reappearing on the hill behind the small grove of oaks.

"Follow him quietly. I'll track." Travis said, motioning to Garrett. "Watch out for darts. Brogan and Liam, take Charlie inside. We'll be back in a couple of hours."

"Hell no!" I leaped away from the group, but not fast enough. The blond giants had their big paws wrapped around my arms before I could take a second step. *Fucking bastards!* "Travis! Garrett! You will pay for this."

Travis stalked toward me, the power of the alpha rippling from his skin. "You will do this," he growled. "I cannot focus on the soldiers and you at the same time. Go with Liam and Brogan. Do not leave their side. For. Anything."

My wolf wanted to roll on its back and show my belly. Going against a direct alpha order was like trying to make yourself jump into a vat of molten steel. It just wouldn't happen.

I stared at the ground, refusing to look him in the eye.

"Do you understand, Charlotte?"

Charlotte? He used my full name. He'd never called me Charlotte. I looked up and saw the pain... the fear he'd spoken of. He knew he was cheating by using the alpha magick to exact obedience, but I understood. And it was enough to forgive him. And Garrett.

"Yes."

Garrett kissed my forehead and whispered that he loved me in my ear before running after Travis, Maddock, and Douglas.

"I love you both, too, you big idiots." It wasn't more than a whisper, but they both turned after I spoke and looked at me for a moment before continuing after the spying soldier. Their focus was on tracking, but they had been listening.

They'd always listened to me. Anything and everything.

They'd left Ada when I told them to go.

Came back when I called.

Fought for me.

Stood by me.

Loved me.

Tears ran down my cheeks, and I covered my mouth to muffle a sob. I didn't want to lose them. What would I do without them? I loved them so much. If I'd just left when Victor tried to take the pack over, we'd be safe in Sanctuary.

But where would my pack be?

Dead?

Or worse?

"It'll be alright, darling," Brogan said, putting a gentle hand against the small of my back. "Let's find you something to sip on. Maddock and Douglas won't let anything happen to your boys. Gods, Douglas by himself could slaughter a whole army."

"He seems a little on the scary side," I admitted between sobs.

Brogan's lips pushed out as he thought about my statement. "He hasn't had the easiest life and has learned to channel his pain against those who deserve it."

"He kills people."

"Yep," Liam said, opening the door for me. "But only people who deserve it."

Somehow, even with both of them assuring me of Travis and Garrett's supposed safety, I still worried.

"I need them to come back." I said as they led me through the foyer into the living room. People stood to the side, silent as we walked through, but the looks they gave Brogan and Liam were dagger sharp.

"They will. Where's your room? You look like you could lie down for a few minutes."

Crawley entered the living room from the kitchen. "Charlie, I—I was only—"

"It's fine, Crawley. It's not your fault. If I hadn't gone out the window, I would've clawed a hole in the wall."

He nodded, but I could feel his guilt weighing him down. His alphas had entrusted him with their most precious possession, and I'd slipped through his fingers.

I approached him and placed a hand on his arm. "I'm sorry. I promise not to run again." It was nice to have someone in the pack trust me and my mates. His loyalty through this transition had made everything just a little easier.

He nodded and stepped to the side so I could continue up the stairs. "You go with her. I'll bring some food up."

The men exchanged a few more words, but I just wanted to rest, like Brogan said. I wanted to try and forget that Travis and Garrett were out there with those crazy Lycan soldiers. My feet climbed the stairs, plodding forward until I reached the top.

I opened my door and walked to the bed. Rubbing my

heels together, I worked the combat boots off without reaching down for them. They clunked to the floor. One loud thump followed by another echoed through the empty room.

My mates' voices were present in my mind—their whispered words of adorations and shouts of my name as they filled me, body and soul. "Come back to me," I whispered, lying back on the bed and snuggling into the pillows coated in their scent.

CHAPTER
THIRTY-ONE

GARRETT

We followed on foot, just far enough back that the soldier wouldn't be suspicious. When we reached a small house about four miles from the lodge, I looked at Travis and frowned. A dozen vans and trucks were scattered around the front, but I counted only six heartbeats. *Where were the rest?* The windows were boarded over, but that wouldn't hinder my ability to hear inside.

Travis waved to Douglas and Maddock. They turned away and circled around the house so that we approached from four different directions.

I held up my hand, signaling everyone to stop. Their voices were loud, and they boasted about their plan to take down the Mason pack once and for all and how pleased Xerxes would be that they were taking down some of Sanctuary's residents in the process.

They were proud of it. Happy they had a hand in slaughtering innocent people. Their species.

Travis signaled for my attention, but didn't speak. If we could hear them, they would be able to hear us if we weren't careful.

"Are they all in the lodge?" one male voice asked.

"Except for the four outside that followed me," another voice answered.

Travis stood from his crouched position, followed by myself, Douglas and Maddock.

"Shit," I muttered. Douglas and Maddock moved toward Travis, and I did the same. We converged on the lawn, only a few feet from each other, as the front door opened and the six Lycans inside came out one at a time as if they had all the time in the world and weren't concerned at all that we were ready to tear them to shreds. But mostly my gut was screaming to know where the rest of the group was hiding. Were they surrounding us? I couldn't hear them. Smell them. Nothing.

My wolf paced, eager to fight and mad as hell that they'd threatened our mate. The alpha bond between Travis and I pulsed with energy, but he didn't move, so neither did the rest of us. We all waited for his lead.

"We're supposed to offer you a chance to come over to our side," one of the largest Lycans said, his voice full of confidence. "Thanks for showing up."

His disdain made me swallow nervously. It was all too easy. Too lackadaisical.

"Are you in charge?" Travis asked, his voice low and calculated. Douglas and Maddock were pretending to pay attention, but I knew they were completely focused on the fields, watching for even the smallest movement. If they had us surrounded already, though, we were dead.

Six we could take. But more tipped the scales in their favor. I couldn't imagine not returning to Charlotte. It was the worst feeling I'd ever encountered, seconded only by the memory of watching my parents murdered by their neighbors.

"I am right now," the man answered.

Wrong answer. My heart beat faster, and every muscle in my body tensed. If he wasn't truly in charge, who was? And where were they?

"Travis," I hissed. "The lodge."

His eyes widened as realization struck us both at the same time. It'd been a ruse the whole time. They'd purposefully tried to lure us away from the lodge, leaving them with fewer guards, and it had worked. *Fuck.* We'd walked right into it.

"Kill?" Douglas whispered, taking a step toward the group of men who didn't deserve to be a Lycan. No matter the pack, Lycans protected each other. The old families would've been horrified by such a lack of loyalty.

"Yes, Douglas," Travis answered.

The mercenary soldiers lunged first, but we were only a split second later. Six to four were decent odds, especially since we had Douglas. His roar gave the hair on the back of my neck a reason to stand on end. If they weren't shitting bricks at the sound, they would be soon enough. We were all seasoned fighters, but Douglas was fifty shades of crazy along with being a skilled soldier.

They drew handguns and fired off maybe one round each, hitting nothing. Within seconds, we'd disarmed them, and the guns lay scattered in pieces on the dusty grass. Douglas broke one guy's neck in less than five seconds. I didn't see it, but I heard his roar of victory and the distinct sound of vertebrae cracking.

He was a beast on the battlefield. An angry fucking beast who, at home, loved to hold newborn babies and sing them to sleep. He said he never got to hold his first-born. His wife was killed while she was still pregnant. Most of us attributed that loss to his ferocity.

Travis said Rose gave him a house in Sanctuary years ago. His job was training the younger generations in fighting skills. But Travis said he doted on children every spare minute he had. Babies especially. Any mother desperate for a few minutes' rest knew they could call Douglas. He had the touch. There wasn't a baby in town that hadn't been soothed to sleep by that man.

But he refused to date or even consider the possibility of finding another mate. He just said Mira was the only one and walked away anytime the subject was broached.

A rush of air across my face brought me back to the present. The guy lunging at me swung another right hook, but I caught his jaw with my fist first, sending him hurtling backward onto the old farmhouse porch. The steps creaked as I clambered up after him. I knelt over him, straddling his body and beat his face until I couldn't see it any longer. There was only redness and swollen mounds of flesh. I grabbed his head and twisted violently, taking pleasure in knowing he would never threaten another Lycan.

Something struck me hard in the center of my back, and I heard Travis snarl as I peeled myself off the crusty, boarded up window. Blood trickled down my face where the exposed nails had torn the skin on my cheek. The pain was slight at first, but then it burned with a sting beyond the damage inflicted. I hated facial wounds.

Wood crashed, and an entire section of the porch collapsed as Travis threw the guy who'd kicked me into a support beam. The dude went straight through it and landed on the grass in front of Douglas. Splinters and shingles rained down beside him.

"No, no, no!" the coward shrieked, trying to climb to his feet and run, but Douglas grabbed his arm and twisted. The snap and crunch was as painful to hear as the man's scream of agony. But they had tricked us and kept us from returning to our mate. They deserved every bit of pain we could dish out and more. They were traitors to their species.

"They're all dead," Douglas announced.

"Let's go!" Travis shouted.

I leaped from the porch, and we took off over the hill. Even at a dead run, it would take us at least twenty minutes to get back. Right now she was safe. I could feel our link. She wasn't scared or in pain.

But that could change at any moment.

CHAPTER
THIRTY-TWO

XERXES

She bowed. "Everything is set. The alphas and their men south are already inside the WR as migrating citizens. They merely await your command to cross the Roosevelt Bridge and move in on the White House. Apparently, the capital is not heavily guarded, only the borders of the Republic."

I smiled. "Let's go watch."

Her eyes widened. "Watch, sir?"

I snapped my fingers, and two Djinn appeared through French doors that led into a small library. "Top of the Eisenhower building next to the White House." A few seconds later, Manda and I were standing in a dark corner on the roof of the building next door to the iconic White House.

A cool breeze whipped through the flags along the capital garden. The blue field and five white stars represented the five major cities of the WR. No states, just metropolises that were filled with wealthy people hoping their advanced technology would keep them safe.

The White House had once been a symbol of freedom to all people in this country. Now it was just headquarters for one of the five Republics that the United States had broken into after the Riots. Of course, the Washington Republic liked to think of itself as better than the others because they took the nation's previous capital and had more money and technology than they could realistically control. In all reality, none of the Republics were any more powerful than the next. They all had reasons for where the lines were drawn and who had stepped into power over the years.

Now it was time for a change. Because the supernatural leaders in Europe, England, and Asia had chosen to stay out of what they called "growth spurts of a baby country," I had free reign to steal power right from under their noses. By the time they realized what I would accomplish, it would be too late. I would control what had once been a superpower on Earth, and under my instruction, it would soon be again.

"Go give the order. Then return immediately. We will watch it fall together."

Manda nodded, and the Djinn holding her arm blinked her away. Less than a minute passed before they returned.

Fifteen minutes later, I saw the first shadow on the White House lawn. It was followed by a dozen more and then another unit and another. No alarms had been tripped yet, and I watched with delight as my Lycan soldiers descended on the White House with a vengeance only a jilted supernatural could sympathize with. The guards never stood a chance, and neither did the man who called himself president of the Washington Republic.

An alarm blared for nearly thirty seconds, but was cut off abruptly as my men entered the White House. A few dozen screams split the air then stopped. The house and the surrounding area was silent as if nothing had happened.

As if I'd not just taken control of the Washington Republic's capital and killed their president.

"One by one, they will fall. And brick by brick, I will have everything."

"People will always fight you, Xerxes," Manda said, holding her head up. She stared at the White House, her shoulders back and her voice calculated, reminding me of the old Mandana Farrok. How she'd fought for her people until I'd taken everything away from her, person by person.

"And they will lose," I answered.

"But you will never find peace."

A snarl ripped from my throat, and I reached for her neck with my hand, wrapping my fingers around her neck and squeezing until she gasped for breath. "I'm not looking for peace. I'm looking for revenge." I waved my hand through the air, gesturing to the city around us. "All of this is merely a means to an end. The only woman I loved was stolen by my people. My own brother helped.

Then the Drakonae stole the Veil from beneath our noses. There is no peace for me in this world or the next. But I will make them all pay for what they did. Every last one of them."

She clawed at my hand for a moment and then stopped.

I squeezed harder, but not enough to do more than leave a nasty bruise. When the light in her eyes started to fade, I released her. She stumbled back a couple of steps and turned to run, but one of the guards caught her arm before she went farther.

"You try to run, Manda, but you have nowhere to go."

"She will find you," Manda hissed, struggling against the guard.

I laughed. "Your mother has been locked away for thousands of years. She's in a big scary world she knows nothing about. It's only a matter of time before my scouts find her and bring her back."

"You'll burn in Drakonae fire one day, Xerxes!" she screamed.

"Take her back to the mansion."

The Djinn soldier saluted and then blinked away with Manda still struggling in his grasp. He wouldn't let her go. They knew my wrath for making mistakes and none of them wanted to pay that price. I made sure everyone knew what I'd done to Manda. And that it would happen to every single one of them, or worse, if they were not flawlessly obedient.

One of my Lycan soldiers exited the White House front entrance and gave the all clear.

"To the front," I said, reaching for the arm of the Djinn guard on my right.

He nodded, and a second later, we were stepping through a vortex and reappearing on the manicured lawn just outside the front door of the White House. He released me as we re-materialized, and the man who'd given the all-clear saluted.

"General Xerxes, the White House has been taken. The president, director of defense, and other heads of the major metropolises were all in session. We have the room waiting for you."

General. I liked the sound of that. I hadn't taken an official title yet, but that one sounded pleasant to the ear. "Just General; do not use my name."

"Yes, General, sir." The Lycan saluted again and took a step backward. He gestured to the door. "Please follow me."

We strolled through the massive doors into an equally impressive foyer. The house was a beautiful mixture of architecture and had been maintained by the WR quite well. The floor shone, and the walls were spotless and filled with paintings from around the world, collected by men decades before the Riots closed the United States borders. Military personnel were allowed access to aircraft and ships, but no private citizens were granted permission to leave or enter the country.

When the borders closed fifty years ago, whoever was inside the country was trapped and whoever had been abroad never came back. Most thought they were the lucky ones.

I smiled as we climbed a large central staircase. They

probably were the lucky ones. The rest of the world had avoided the political upheaval and social backsliding at the announcement that supernatural creatures lived on earth.

Armed Lycans lined the hallways. We turned a corner, and I saw blood on the floor and a stack of bodies beyond the smear. Another door was opened, and I found myself at the head of large conference room. Men sat silently around the table. Some were old. Some younger. But they were all running on pure adrenaline. The speed of their pulses raised mine in delight.

My army hadn't killed them all, which meant I would get the pleasure of ending their lives one-by-one. The ultimate victory over the WR would personally belong to me.

I walked to the head of the table and sat in the single, empty high-backed chair. "I love what you've done with the place. It's been nearly a century since I visited the White House."

My gaze descended on the man opposite me at the far end of the table. His hair was cut short, and he wore the blue uniform of the WR military. His bright eyes flashed in anger, but not fear like the rest of the men seated along the sides of the table.

"I don't know how you got through our border scans, but you better leave the same way you came. When the army realizes what you've done, you will die and so will all of your men."

I lifted one hand from my lap and gestured toward one of the men seated closest to me. My magic flowed forward, wrapping steely tendrils around the poor bastard's neck. I made a fist and his neck snapped, his body falling forward in a haphazard fashion.

The other men at the table took a collective swallow, but none moved from their seats. They knew their fate and were brave to not flee from it –resigned to the fact that they were all about to breathe their last.

CHAPTER
THIRTY-THREE

CHARLIE

"There are strange people outside chanting." Brogan entered my room and walked to the window. He pushed aside the curtains, and I opened an eyeball to look at him.

"How long was I asleep?" I rolled over and saw an untouched tray of food on my nightstand. Grabbing the glass of water, I downed half before climbing out of my soft bed. The chanting was loud, but in a language I didn't recognize.

"Do you know what they are saying?" I asked, joining him beside the window and peering down at the parking lot. Several people in black robes were spread across the parking lot... in fact—I pushed my face against the glass—it looked like they might be around the entire lodge.

"How long was I out?"

"Only thirty minutes or so. Not long," he replied. "I

don't know what they are saying, but it sounds like witchcraft."

It did indeed, and that was bad. The last time Xerxes and witches mixed, half of my pack died. "We have to stop them. Whatever it is, it's not good."

He nodded. "I'll get Liam," he said, leaving my side at the window.

I craned my neck, trying to get a better look, but when my nose touched the glass a second time, it electrocuted me and I saw a flash of red shoot across the window.

"Fucking hell," Brogan shouted, doubled over next to my doorway. He sucked in a quick breath and straightened to his full height.

"What is it?" I hurried to his side.

"I can't leave. It's like there's a barrier across the door."

"But it's open," I said, picking up a shoe from beside my bed and tossing it at the open doorway. The invisible barrier lit up, scorching the bottom of the shoe before it fell to the floor—still inside my bedroom.

We can't get out.

"Brogan?" Liam's voice called from down the hallway at the base of the stairs.

Brogan moved closer to the doorway, but didn't dare touch the electric barrier again. "Yeah? Where are you stuck?"

"I'm with several people down in the living area, but we can't cross through the doorway into the kitchen, much less the doors leading outside."

"The windows are hot, too. Be sure and tell everyone not to touch them."

"Will do," Liam hollered.

I looked up at Brogan and trembled. What the hell was going on?

Screams erupted downstairs, and we both rushed for the doorway, barely stopping before colliding with the invisible barrier. Brogan picked up an umbrella propped against the wall and poked it at the door. The electricity zapped through the umbrella, and he cursed again, throwing the umbrella across the room.

More screams. Then the word "fire" filtered up the stairs.

"Liam!" Brogan shouted.

No response. Just more screams.

A thump on the roof above us gave me goosebumps. Then another crash sounded downstairs, and I nearly jumped out of my skin when a flaming jar flew through the window in my bedroom. It exploded, sending the burning contents spraying through the rooms.

The flames grew quickly, and I coughed, covering my mouth with the neck of my shirt. Brogan lunged toward the bathroom only to curse profusely when the barrier in the doorway between the rooms zapped him, sending him stumbling backward.

"Are you okay?"

"Yeah," he groaned. "It's blocked every doorway. The inside ones, too. We can't get to the bathroom away from this fire."

That meant we couldn't wet down anything. If we couldn't get out, the smoke could kill us before the fire did. I could already feel the burn in the pit of my lungs.

I approached the broken window and stared out. The witches remained in a circle, and soldiers gathered behind their ring, continuing to throw Molotov jars at the lodge. Tears welled in my eyes, as much from the smoke building in the room as the pain in my heart. I counted for ten seconds, and five more jars sailed through the air, landing against or on the lodge. And those were only the ones I could see from my window.

The whole building must look like one big ball of flame, meaning Travis and Garrett were either dead or on their way. The smoke had to be hundreds of feet in the air.

I coughed again and squinted. Smoke was clouding the room faster than it should've. Staring at the doorway I saw the problem: the smoke was trapped inside the barrier just like we were. *Nothing* could pass through. Not even air?

"It's not filtering out," I said.

"What?" he asked, coughing into his arm.

"The smoke isn't leaving the room. Not through the door, not back out the window. We should be able to breathe fresh air through this hole." I shook my head. "There's nothing. The smoke just bounces off the hole."

"Fuck," he growled. He walked toward a wall and reached out gingerly. I cringed, waiting for the barrier to send a shock through him. Nothing happened. His hand rested safely against the sheetrock wall. He turned his head and caught my gaze.

We were both wondering the same thing. Did the barrier extend beyond the doors and windows?

He pulled back his fist and punched through the wall. No outcry. No zap of energy. Again and again, he punched until his arm went all the way through. Then he pressed his mouth to the hole and breathed deeply.

I hurried to his side, avoiding the spots where the fire had caught on the floor rug. At least the hardwood floors were slowing the spread or we'd be crispy already.

"Breathe through here," he said, catching my arm and pulling me closer. My body was plastered to his a second later, and our faces shared intimate space in front of the hole in the wall, but when the fresh clean air hit my lungs, I didn't care anymore.

"How is it so clear?"

"Liam said he couldn't come up the stairs, so that means it's completely sealed. There's no window on the hallway, so there's nowhere for them to throw one through."

"Liam," he yelled, but only a hoarse croak emerged; even with the fresh air, the smoke had already taken a heavy toll. "Punch a wall out into a sealed room for clean air. A closet. Anything."

Through the pandemonium of screaming and crying, I couldn't hear him respond. "Did you hear him?"

He shook his head, the movement nudging my cheek.

A terrified scream pierced the air. I couldn't tell who it was until she cried out my name. "Charlie, save my baby. Please. Karly is upstairs. If you can get her, please." Then her words changed to screams of pain, and I tried to choke back the sobs. I couldn't afford to waste our air.

"Can we make the hole big enough for me to fit through? Her baby is down the hallway."

He pushed me backward and then began yanking out

chunks of sheetrock and insulation. Within a few moments, he had squeezed his huge frame through the newly enlarged hole. I followed easily and pointed down the hall to the right.

"The room with the pink door."

"Which wall?"

I stood in front of the door for a second and thought about the room. "Here," I said, pointing to the left side. "Can you hear a heartbeat?"

He shook his head. "Too many screams from downstairs." Rearing back, he kicked the wall, using his steel-toed boot like a sledgehammer. Pieces of the wall shattered, leaving a nice-sized hole, and I touched his arm to stop him from kicking again.

"I can fit," I said, leaning down and slithering through the opening.

The room was filled with smoke, and the carpet in the center burned bright, but the crib was against the hall wall, and Karly was still alive! Her little coughs filled me with hope. I leaned over and snatched her from the crib and thrust her through the opening into Brogan's arms. A crash behind me sent me hurtling through the hole back into the hallway. Another Molotov had exploded inside the baby's bedroom. We'd gotten there just in time.

"Are there more kids up here? Or anyone?"

"There could be. We have to check."

He drew in a deep breath and nodded. "Take the baby and stay in the center of the hallway where there's more air for her. She's got bad smoke inhalation. And stay low, the smoke is starting to creep through these holes."

I dropped to the floor with Karly snuggled tightly against my chest. The little girl was only fifteen months old. Her daddy had been killed at the Vicksburg Bridge. Tears streamed down my eyes.

I'd been worried the soldiers would execute the pack, but I'd never dreamed they'd try to burn us alive. How could Victor go along with this; surely he wouldn't stand by and watch his family tortured and killed?

"Found another one!" Brogan's big voice boomed through the hallway, and his feet pounded toward me, vibrating the floor.

The baby he thrust into my arms was Isis, Sheila's little girl. She was almost three.

"Charlie, mama is hurt."

I hugged her to my body next to Karly and looked up at Brogan.

He shook his head. "I think the barrier killed her. She must've kept hitting it or fallen against it. I don't know. There's nothing I can do for her. I can't even get her body."

Tears flowed down my cheeks, and I nodded. "It's okay, honey. Auntie Charlie has you. I won't let anything happen, okay."

"Mama's hurt," the little girl sobbed. "Fire is bad," she coughed out.

"Mama is gone, sweet girl. She's gone to the stars with our ancestors. She isn't hurting any more. I promise."

My chest tightened, and I gasped for a breath before turning to Brogan. "Did you check the others yet?"

He knelt down to the floor beside me and nodded. "These two were the only ones alive."

I hyperventilated a few breaths before I put a lid on

the grief that wanted to come pouring out. But it wouldn't help these babies for me to lose it now.

"Can't we punch out through an outside wall?"

"I already tried. The outside wall is charged with the energy barrier. Every time I touch it, it's worse. I felt my heart stop for a second this last time," he answered.

"Do you think they are okay downstairs? I haven't heard much lately, and the fire is burning so loudly. It's like a roar in my ears."

"I don't know. I hope so," he answered. "Let me hold the toddler." He reached for Isis and peeled her off my neck, transferring her to his. She latched right on and continued to sob into his shoulder. I readjusted the baby and leaned against his massive frame. The cracking and creaking above us signaled our imminent doom.

We just sat in the center of the hallway.

Praying.

CHAPTER
THIRTY-FOUR

TRAVIS

I cleared the last hill before we reached the lodge and shouted in agony at the sight. My heart clenched inside my ribcage. The whole building shimmered in a strange red bubble and was burning inside it. I could see flames through the broken windows. But there was no smoke trailing into the sky. The barrier trapped it all inside with...

"Charlie!" My chest collapsed on itself, and I couldn't draw a breath. Garrett cursed, but kept running.

"Come on. You can feel her, just like me. She's not dead."

He was right. But she was close. I could sense her fear and her struggle to breathe. The choking sensation was overwhelming.

Anger swelled past the fear, and I snarled. "Kill them all!" I ordered as Douglas and Maddock caught up to me.

They nodded and followed me as I ran down the hillside, following Garrett.

If anyone was going to get out of that lodge alive, those witches needed to die. How the hell had Xerxes dug up that many of them, anyway? There weren't that many family lines left after all these millennia. He had to have been collecting them for decades. *Gods, those poor women.*

The four of us approached a small group of soldiers from behind and tore into them before they were able to draw a single weapon. Necks snapped. Throats were ripped. Whatever was fastest. Douglas' face and hands were covered in blood, and the golden light in his eyes read absolute pleasure. While I felt disgust for the wasted lives, he hungered for more blood to be spilled.

"The witches, Douglas."

He nodded and darted off, slinking up to one and then another, the shadow of death incarnate. They dropped silently one by one, dead before they even knew what touched them.

We turned our focus on the next group of unaware soldiers. They were so engrossed in what they were doing they didn't see or hear us approaching.

"Hey," Maddock said, pointing at a body a few feet away. "You know this guy? We didn't kill him. There's a bullet in his heart."

I moved slowly toward the stench of death and nodded when his face came into view. "Victor. He was the man who sold them out."

Maddock frowned. "Guess he got what was coming to him then."

"The barrier is failing!" The call went up from the other side of the lodge, but it was enough to give me hope. Douglas was making a significant dent in the witch population. We were only a few yards from the next group of soldiers and their crates of Molotov cocktails. *Bastards.* Trapping women and children and burning them to death. *We don't live in the Dark Ages!*

My fingers curled, claws extending as parts of me shifted while the rest remained in human form. Years of fighting taught me to take every advantage of my supernatural DNA. These weren't just human soldiers trying to kill supernaturals. These were Lycans turning on their own kind.

They deserved no mercy.

Garrett, Maddock, and I lunged at the same time. Blood spewed from their traitorous bodies, and again, all five were dead and spread across the grass in a sea of red before a single man could utter a word.

We rushed to the other side of the house to find Douglas with his mouth on the throat of one Lycan while he held another in his grasp whimpering and begging for his life. A pathetic excuse for a man who knew he'd chosen the wrong side of things.

Douglas looked up at me, dropped the body from his jaws, and smiled. "The barrier is down. They are all dead." His jaws had morphed back to human, and his fangs retreated, but almost his whole body was coated in a layer of blood and human tissue. He pulled the last soldier close to his body and then shoved him down over his knee. The crack of the man's spine resonated inside my body, but it was justice. Then Douglas drove his hand into the man's chest and ripped out his heart.

Any Lycan could regenerate from broken bones and most wounds, but losing a heart was an injury that I'd never seen any being, supernatural or otherwise, recover from. Lycan power resided in blood. It healed from the inside out. But if an injury drained too much blood…it meant the end.

"Travis!" Garrett shouted from the edge of the burning porch. "Can you see a way in?"

I backed up a few steps and took in the gut-wrenching sight. The whole building was in flames. With the barrier down, smoke billowed hundreds of feet into the sky, telling everyone for miles around that death had arrived.

"We need help. It's too hot to get inside. The air is extra hot from when that fucking barrier was up!" Garrett shouted again, taking a hesitant step away from the burning front door.

"Charlie is alive. Several other are, too. Focus. Figure out where."

A window shattered above our heads, and Brogan's head popped out between the flames. He coughed and gasped for air. "Catch. I've got two babies coming out."

"Where's Charlie?"

"She's here. She refuses to jump until the babies are out." He picked up a small body and hurled it through the air.

I jumped to the side, catching the infant as gently as possible in my arms. Its pulse was weak, but it was alive.

"Give it to me," Douglas growled, appearing at my side as if from thin air.

I nodded and handed the baby to him before seeing Garrett catch the next child hurled from the upstairs window. He caught the slightly larger child, swinging his arms in motion with the child's flight to lessen the jolt of being caught.

"Here she comes!" Brogan shouted.

Charlie's dark hair whipped around her head. Her face was red, and her heart beat sluggishly. She couldn't possibly have the strength to jump. Her legs trembled as she climbed onto the windowsill.

Time slowed as her legs extended, pushing herself away from the window and into the open air. Flames licked at the edges of the window, and Brogan hurried to follow her.

I moved to break her fall and caught the brunt of her weight before it slammed into the hard earth. We fell to the ground together. Brogan hit the ground a few feet away, the heavy thud vibrating through my body as I wrapped my arms around Charlie and crawled to my feet. Carrying her tucked close against me, I moved away from the burning building and set her down next to Douglas and the two children he was calming with an old Celtic lullaby.

Garrett was next to me as we checked over Charlie's body for injury.

"I'm fine. You have to get the others," she said, coughing through each word. "They are trapped on the bottom floor."

I stood and looked to Maddock. He was close to the front door, but flames covered the door and the walls.

Windows were exploding all around the lodge, sending shards of glass flying out at us.

"You have to get them out!" She shoved our hands away and tried to stand.

"Stay," I growled. "We'll find them." I didn't know how, but I wasn't about to let her go back into that inferno.

"We could hear some beneath us in the hallway. Try the back wall. The dining room."

I nodded, and the three of us took off around the building. The bodies of the witches Douglas had killed stared at us as we passed them, their blank eyes surely a warning of the inevitable that lay ahead.

We rounded the corner and saw what none of us could've hoped for. People crawling out of one of the back windows. Racing forward, we helped one after the other to the safety of the grass, away from the building. Liam stood just behind the window as I approached to help another woman.

"Took you guys long enough to kill those bitches," Liam grumbled. He put his hands on the windowsill and leapt through the opening onto the porch. The small explosion following him made both of us run a little faster.

The second floor collapsed in onto the first, sending a boom vibrating through our bodies. The whole middle of the lodge fell in on itself, but all I could hear was Charlie's scream from the front.

I pushed reassurances through our bond and felt her fear subside slightly. We each took a couple of people, draping their arms over our shoulders. Together we helped them stumble around to the front as they fought to clear their lungs of the smoke they'd taken in. Their Lycan DNA would mend their lungs in the next few hours, but presently, they were weak and vulnerable. We needed to get to a safe place.

We needed to get them to Sanctuary.

CHAPTER
THIRTY-FIVE

GARRETT

"We must get away from this building. The military and fire rescue has to be on their way. The rising smoke can be seen for miles," I said, kneeling at Charlie's side. I rubbed her back as she coughed. It would be at least a couple of hours before her lungs were healed from the burn of the smoke.

Douglas stood and handed off the infant he'd been holding to Maddock. "I'll make sure the bodies are gone."

"I'll help you, Douglas," Travis said, rising from beside Charlie.

They walked toward the burning lodge. Douglas picked up a large rock from the ground and hurled it at a front window. It shattered into a thousand pieces, and they worked swiftly, tossing body after body into the lodge.

The fire wouldn't hide their deaths, but it would conceal most of the evidence.

I stared a few moments longer before dragging my attention back to the group surrounding me. "Let's try to move to that big tree about a quarter mile down the road."

The group rose; those of us without injury helped the ones struggling to breathe. Ten minutes later, after a great deal of heavy lifting, Charlie was settled with the two children against the trunk of the massive oak. Crawley and the four females Liam had helped survive the fire huddled together a few feet from her. They were it. They were all that remained of the Mason pack.

After all the fighting and arguing, Xerxes won anyway. He'd managed to wipe out one of the most powerful packs to survive the Riots intact. The Masons had been a beacon to those trapped in the intolerant Republics. Without them, there were none to help.

Xerxes would decimate the packs left in the SECR and the WR. Packs remaining on the West Coast had a chance, at least, if they didn't believe Xerxes' messengers being sent to convince them otherwise. There was more than enough hate to go around. It wouldn't be hard for Xerxes to trick more Lycans into an alliance.

The branches parted. Travis and Douglas slipped between the boughs and sank to the ground next to Liam and myself.

"How is she?" Travis asked.

"Tired, but healing," I answered. "They are sleeping."

Travis nodded. "The fire department was arriving just as we lit out of there."

"They didn't see you?" I asked, nerves making my skin crawl. The last thing we needed was a bunch of humans hauling us in for questioning or arresting us.

Douglas shook his head. "No one saw us. They were too focused on the billowing fire and smoke cloud ahead of them. We circled around the side, through some brush, and then to here."

A ding sounded from Travis' pocket. He pulled out his cell phone and swiped the screen. "Text from Rose. They are about two hours away." His fingers tapped the screen as he wrote back. "I told them where we were and to avoid the lodge," he said, tucking the phone back into his pants pocket.

Home. I hadn't called Sanctuary home for long, but it was exactly that. *Home.* Since the Riots, I'd moved from place to place. Military station to military station. Never staying grounded for more than a few months at a time. Certainly never growing roots or thinking about looking for a mate to start a family. Now, I had both. My brother back in my life. A mate to share with him. And the possibility of actually having a family in a home.

Sanctuary was filled with supernaturals who lived together without fighting. Everyone had responsibilities, and everyone played by the rules. Rose wasn't really someone you could fuck with and stay alive to talk about it. The Lycans in town had an elected alpha pair to help with organization and petty argument solving, but Rose was the Sentinel. Most Lycans just regarded her as the supreme alpha.

Nothing happened in town that she didn't know about or approve.

Engines rumbled on the road a dozen yards from the tree. I watched through the branches as several police cars rolled slowly, making their way toward the burning lodge. No one made a sound, and no one moved. Ada was in the Texas Republic, but the local police were not particularly "Other" friendly. The military courted us and did everything they could to recruit us to their ranks, but the local towns and police departments continued to blame us for anything and everything that ever went wrong.

Even so, it was better here than anywhere else in the former United States. All other Republics shot and killed Others on sight. Hunting us for sport was also encouraged.

The tires crunched on the dirt and gravel road. The sounds were as loud for me as if I'd been standing two feet away instead of almost forty. I could hear their radio conversations as well as everyone else in our group.

We all sat, barely breathing. Waiting. Just waiting for the cop to continue down the road so we could all gasp for the air we were denying ourselves.

Several hours passed before the sound of two engines pulled my focus from the steady rise and fall of Charlie's chest. I kept watching and listening. We'd come so close to losing her, and my wolf was desperate to feel her wrapped tightly in my arms again.

The vision of her holding the two babies was almost too much to take in. None of the four females sitting with Crawley had claimed the babies. My heart hurt for those little ones and wondered what Charlie would do with them long term. A large part of me wanted to tell her we'd keep them. But I couldn't say that without at least speaking to Travis first.

She was the one and only love of my life. Of this I was certain. But she was more than just mine. She was Travis' mate as well. In all things, we were a team. If she decided to keep the children, I knew neither Travis nor myself would attempt to remove them from her care. They would be ours as well.

Children were precious, especially Lycan children who were blessings from the gods. Their parents had died fighting to keep them alive. Both of them would grow up knowing the stories of their courageous parents, no matter if we kept them or they went to another Lycan family.

I caught Travis' gaze, and he nodded. He'd felt the rush of protective instinct surrounding my thoughts over the children. Charlotte looked up at us both and mouthed '*Thank you*.'

In that instant, I knew we'd become a family of five.

A buzz came from Travis' pocket, and he pulled out his phone again. "They are pulling around. We need to load into the SUVs as fast as possible. Still a few police cars roaming the area."

Everyone stood. Douglas and Maddock helped as many as they could. Liam and Brogan pushed apart the branches, and we made a beeline for the SUVs. I tucked Charlotte against my chest and took one of the children from her arms as we walked together.

Mikjáll jumped out of one SUV and helped load in two of the females from the lodge that Douglas had draped around him. The other two were helped by Alek and Jared into the other vehicle.

"Hurry," Mikjáll growled. "There are more vehicles coming this way."

Crawley got in first and took the children, one-by-one, from Charlotte, and then I lifted her up into the captain chair next to the door and climbed in after her. I saw Travis through the windshield as he climbed into the SUV in front of us.

Alek Melos, a Gryphon and sheriff of Sanctuary, rounded the hood and slid into the driver's seat. We were moving a few seconds later.

"What happened?" Alek asked from the front seat.

My body swayed with each bump in the road. I knelt on the floor and sighed. "Xerxes."

The car warmed ten degrees almost instantly. Mikjáll's eyes burned bright orange, and he looked over his shoulder at me.

"Hey, dude. Enough with the sauna," Alek said, whacking the dragon on the upper arm.

A snarl exploded from the young Drakonae, but his eyes darkened to normal, and the temperature in the vehicle returned to non-steamy.

"Xerxes was in Texas?" Mikjáll asked.

I met his angry gaze and shook my head. "He's recruiting Lycans and witches. They lured us away from the lodge. Before we realized what was happening, it was too late to save most of the Mason pack."

"I'm so sorry, Charlie," Calliope called from the very back of the vehicle. I looked behind me but couldn't see her over the bench in the back.

Charlie sniffled, but didn't speak. She clutched the toddler to her breast and turned to stare out the window at the passing landscape.

I put a hand on her thigh, but there was no response. She just sat there, her broken heart bleeding through our bond. I hadn't cried once in my life, but the pain pouring out of her was enough to make my eyes water.

"Can I hold the baby for you, love?"

She shook her head and tightened her grip on the toddler who cuddled silently in her arms. Douglas held the smaller child, rocking her in his arms. The child was hungry, but Douglas' voice was miraculously keeping her quiet.

"Where is Sochi?" I asked, directing my question to Mikjáll and Alek in the front.

"She's lying back here with me. Pregnant and out cold," Calliope said. "Whatever drugs he had her on are taking forever to leave her system. She opens her eyes every once in a while and asks about a baby. I just tell her she's safe, and we are taking her to Sanctuary. Get some rest, Charlie. Let someone else hold that baby while you close your eyes."

"I'm fine," Charlotte whispered.

Fine was the furthest thing from what she was. Distraught. Angry. Terrified. Those were the emotions flowing through our triad bond. Travis pushed a wave of reassurance through the bond, but it didn't change her state of mind. Her heart still raced, and her breathing stayed erratic.

I wanted nothing more than to soothe away her pain.

We both did. But nothing could be done until we were safely back in Sanctuary. It was too risky to stop on the road in between. Cops liked to poke their noses into everyone's business, and that was something we couldn't have happen.

CHAPTER
THIRTY-SIX

CHARLIE

My pack was gone. Everything was gone. Five people had gotten out. That's all Liam had been able to save. *Five.*

Brogan had thrown the babies to safety. They were sleeping semi-peacefully. The little one, Karly, was starving. I could hear her belly rumbling every few minutes. Still she stayed quiet, like she knew there was nothing we could do. Either that or Douglas, creepy blood-covered-Lycan-warrior-Douglas, had a voice filled with magick. I'd never seen a man take to a child so fondly that wasn't his own.

I clutched Isis to my chest and kissed the top of her head. The toddler's father had died at Vicksburg, and her mother had been lost today in the fire. Isis lost her parents the same way as Karly.

Somehow Travis and Garrett had known I would

keep them. Both of the children. They were my responsibility. The last of the Mason pack's legacy. Both of my mates had given their blessing. The children would remain with us.

"New home?" Isis whispered, laying her chubby hand against the window beside us.

"Yes, baby girl." I stared at the familiar town on the horizon as we approached. The long road wound back and forth between rolling hills. The Blackmoor castle rose high above all the other buildings, a reminder that this was no ordinary small Texas town. Garrett's hand hadn't moved from my leg the entire drive. It was warm and comforting, and I honestly wanted nothing more than to curl up in his arms—in both their arms—and just cry.

I'd failed my pack. Failed my parents. I'd abandoned the lodge where I'd lived for the better part of a century. My home had gone up in puff of smoke. My family.

"Where's my baby? Who are you?" The hysterical wail came from the back of the SUV.

Isis screamed and clutched my neck. Karly cried out as well, and the entire vehicle fell into chaos.

"Please, hon, you're pregnant. We got you away from Xerxes. We are taking you to your sister, Riza."

"My baby! Where's my baby?" The young female Kitsune screamed again, prompting the children to also continue screaming.

"Look, you need to calm down. It's not good for your baby or the children in the car," Calliope snarled.

I'd heard that voice before, and I knew black eyes

came with it. Frightening black eyes that made you want to run for cover. I could tell she wasn't angry, more using the scary voice to shock the young woman out of her hysterics.

It worked.

"Please, miss," the Kitsune said, keeping her voice more level this time. "Please tell me you got Lila out, too. My daughter."

"Another baby? We didn't know there was another. Sochi, I'm sorry." Calliope's voice broke over the last word.

"He still has her." Sochi wept.

My heart broke for her. I hadn't lost a child, but could imagine it was ten times worse than what I'd experienced, and my pain was nearly unbearable.

"Please go back. I can't leave her alone with him."

"We can't go back now," Calliope said. "But I'm sure Rose will come up with a plan to get your daughter back."

The young woman's sobs wrenched at my heart, and I kissed the top of Isis' head again, tasting the smoke and the danger we'd narrowly avoided.

The vehicles stopped, and everyone began climbing out. I handed Isis to Garrett and stepped onto the running bar and then down to the cobblestone road. He placed her back into my outstretched arms and gave me a squeeze.

"I need Karly, too," I said. Douglas had exited the vehicle from the other side, and I couldn't see him. Something inside me refused to be parted from either of them. "Where's Douglas?"

"Right 'ere, lass."

He came up on my right, and I sighed in relief.

"Why don't I take them both into the cafe and get them something to eat and clean up a bit in the back? The pixies can help me while you and yours get situated," he said, holding out an arm for Isis. "Aren't you a bonny thing?" he cooed at the toddler in my arms.

I expected Isis to shrink away from the strange man, but instead, she loosened her grip on my neck and smiled at Douglas.

"Douglas has a gift with babies, Charlotte," Garrett said. "They will be safe with him. I promise."

"Okay," I answered, relinquishing Isis from my arms to Douglas'.

He took her, and they rubbed noses, giggled, and marched down the sidewalk. A moment later, he disappeared with them into the cafe.

People flooded the area. Diana, Miles, and Eli all came from across the circle. Several Lycans had come forward, carrying blankets and stacks of clothes. It was more than we needed, but welcome all the same.

Garrett took a blanket and wrapped it around my shoulders. My shirt was torn, and the wind whipped through it each time a breeze blew.

Travis appeared a second later at my side. Their scents filled my lungs, and I leaned my head against his shoulder and then against Garrett's.

Rose spoke with a couple of Lycans I'd never met before. She gave instructions for housing for those who had survived Ada. The four women asked to share a home and were granted the request. Crawley was offered his own, and he accepted gratefully.

When my pack had been taken care of, Rose approached the three of us. I took a deep breath and waited. The woman exuded power and control. There was nothing on Earth like being in the presence of a Lamassu. Their power flowed from them like a river of magick, rippling through time and space and coating everything around them. But where Xerxes' magick had been cold and sharp, Rose's was warm and inviting.

"I'm so sorry about your loss. But I welcome you into Sanctuary. I hope it will one day mean as much to you as the home your pack occupied in Ada for centuries." Her brown eyes were filled with compassion. She touched my arm, and peace flowed through my body, a cleansing stream of magick. "I know we can't ever replace what you and your pack mates lost, but we will care for and protect you like family. Travis and Garrett are lucky to have you as their mate, Charlotte Mason. Those babies are lucky to have you, as well. I'll send some people by with things you'll need for the house." She looked up at Travis then over at Garrett and winked. "I doubt your place has any baby items."

Travis chuckled. "No, we don't."

"Thank you," I said. "How did you know we were keeping them?"

She met my gaze and smiled. "You hesitated to give them to Douglas. And you watched him until he went inside. Child, they may not be your blood, but you've already adopted them in your heart."

It was true. I could already feel them becoming a part of my soul.

Rose sidestepped suddenly, looking behind Travis.

All three of us turned, but nothing was visible except the empty road leading out of Sanctuary.

"What was it?" Travis asked.

Rose shook her head and frowned. "It was more of a feeling. Something disturbed the field around the town there by the road. But it's gone now. I can't feel it anymore. I'll have the Protectors scout the area."

"A Djinn?" Travis pressed.

"I think so." Rose met my gaze again. "There's nothing to worry about. We have more than enough guards to ward off a single Djinn stupid enough to wander into town. We've been doing it for decades."

I took a deep breath, hoping the safety and peace I felt in this town wasn't a figment of my imagination.

"Mikjáll! Sochi!" Riza shouted as she ran across the circle. She leaped into Mikjáll's arms and gave him a kiss that reminded me how long it'd been since I kissed my mates. She slid from his arms and embraced her sister next, who was being held upright by Liam. The reunion brought tears to my eyes. So much joy over being reunited mixed with the pain of loss, of knowing that Sochi's baby girl was still out there somewhere.

Rose had led them to save that girl. To save all of us. Rose had sent help to save us from Savannah earlier this year as well. This was a place I could be proud to call home. This was a place my parents would've approved of. They wouldn't leave Lila out there for long. They would find a way to rescue the baby, too.

I could be happy here with these people. Loyal. Protective. Generous.

"I saw the two adorable babies Douglas was feeding

in the cafe," Diana said, walking up beside me. "He said they were yours."

Well, maybe walking wasn't correct. The poor Drakonae female looked like a waddling duck.

She grinned and pointed a finger at me. "Don't say it. I know I look like a cow that hasn't been milked in a month."

A small smile tugged at the corners of my mouth. "I didn't say anything."

"I'm glad you're safe. Alek called ahead and said your pack took heavy casualties in a fire. I'm so sorry. May peace fill your soul, my friend." She hugged me, and I felt her belly thump several times against my hip.

"Strong ba—" I paused. "Babies?"

She winked and sighed. "Three. Any day."

"Congratulations."

"I know nothing will ever be Ada, Charlotte, but this town is full of good people who take care of each other. I know you will grow to love this town as much as I have. And I haven't been here that long yet."

"I know. I just..." Tears welled in my eyes, and I rubbed my face, wiping them away. "I'm sorry. I just can't do this right now."

"It is alright, Charlotte. I'll be here for you anytime you need."

"Charlie!" Eira and Killían were approaching from across the circle. "I was so scared when Alek called and said the lodge burned!"

Diana stepped back to stand with her husbands, and Eira moved forward. My friend wrapped her arms around me, and I let the tears flow.

"Five, Eira. Five," I sobbed. "Five people and the two babies, Isis and Karly."

"I know. I couldn't believe it when he said." She leaned back and stared into my eyes. "You are going to survive this, too, Charlotte Mason. We are warriors. Do you hear me? You saved everyone you could. Your parents would be proud."

"I lost almost everyone."

"Xerxes is an evil bastard who deserves to rot in the pits of Tartarus forever. You fought the good fight. And those five people and two little innocent babies are alive because you didn't give up. You are with your mates because you didn't give up."

"Eira is right, Charlotte," Garrett said, slipping his hand around my waist and tucking me closer to his body as my friend took a step back. "You did everything right. You can't blame yourself for the outcome."

I was grateful for my friend's reassurances, but I needed to mourn for what I'd lost. All those people who had died... for Victor's power grabbing. We could've been prepared. Maybe. Maybe not. But at least we could've tried.

But if we'd all been inside when they came, we would've all died. If Travis, Garrett, Maddock, and Douglas hadn't gone hunting for the soldiers, we would've all been trapped together, and we would've all died together.

The alternative was worse than reality.

But the loss of so many still shredded my soul. People continued to die around me. I thought I'd lost everything at Vicksburg. Then Savannah. Then I came back to Ada to have my uncle try to tear away what was left only to have it stripped from me in the end anyway.

Xerxes always won. Death always won.

"Take me home, please," I said, looking up at Garrett and then over at Travis.

They nodded, and we moved away from the crowd.

CHAPTER
THIRTY-SEVEN

XERXES

A knock at the Oval Office door pulled me out of the plans strewn over the desk. "Come in."

A man, a Djinn, walked in a few steps and stood, waiting to be given permission to speak.

"Yes?" I turned the page on a book of maps detailing the layout of the five major cities in the Washington Republic.

"The standing army in New York has surrendered. The commanders await your orders. Should they execute or assimilate the soldiers?" He bowed his head and clasped his hands together in front of him. Silent again, but beneath the surface, he hungered to feed. A trained killer. One of many I'd taught to go out into the world and perpetuate the story that the Djinn were ruthless, psychopathic killers. Everyone feared them, and no one engaged them.

The truth humans would never know was that Djinn

lived and cared for their people just like any other race. So much so that they had lived in complete servitude to me for thousands of years to prevent the deaths of more of their people. Even most supernaturals believed the lies I'd perpetuated. Very few were still alive that remembered the Djinn free from my hand.

"Tell them to line them up, and I want you to kill four men out of every five." Not only would it cripple the morale of the Republic army, it would keep the chance of a rebellion very low. Ordinary citizens were easy to control. Trained soldiers who hated supernatural beings were not.

The Djinn sucked in a quick breath, but I saw a split second glint of pleasure dance across his face. "Yes, General," he answered, his voice calm; I could hear his heart pounding with excitement in his chest. Adrenaline poured out of him, flooding the room with the sweet scent of his bloodlust.

According to my latest update from Manda, the SECR central government officials went into seclusion the second word of my victory in Washington spread. I had hoped to take down both capitals, one after the other, but for now, I would settle for commanding the WR and secretly controlling the SECR until they relaxed their guard and I was able to get all the heads of government together and take them out all at once. Once they were dead, I didn't need that troublesome bitch any longer. The rest of her race responded to threats of being boxed. Manda only responded to me killing her people in front of her.

It grew tiresome, and she would be more trouble than

she was worth once I had complete control of the SECR. And when that happened, I would enjoy killing her very slowly after I killed the rest of her family and court in front of her.

I scribbled the order on a piece of paper and signed it. "Here."

He stepped forward and took the paper. Folding it carefully, he bowed and flashed from the room.

"Cal," I called out.

"Yes, General, sir," another Djinn stepped into the room from the small office adjacent to the Oval.

"Take me to the palace."

The Djinn nodded and stepped forward. He held out his palm, and I laid my hand in his. A moment later, the world folded around me, and we stepped out of the vortex on the other side of the world. The air was warmer, and the noise of the city was gone, replaced by the quiet breeze blowing through the palace halls.

"Remain at the door."

"Yes, General, sir."

I pushed open the doors to my suite and breathed in the rich scent of incense. "Where are my girls?"

The harem door flew open, and my three lovelies ran across the room, dropping to the floor at my feet in a prostrate position, hands above them, palms on the floor, and their foreheads pressed to the carpet.

"Ah, it has been too long." I stripped off my shirt and tossed it onto the satin-covered bed. "Come to me." A sigh slipped from my chest as their hands slid up my legs and removed the rest of my clothing. Lily's mouth settled over my hard dick, and I fisted her hair, fucking her sweet mouth until she gagged. Pulling back a short few moments gave her a breath of air before I went at it again, thrusting until I came down her throat. She swallowed every drop and licked me clean.

"Excellent warm up, Lily." I pointed to the bed, and all three women jumped onto the low-lying mattress. It was time to celebrate my victory with three willing women in my bed who knew everything I liked.

CHAPTER
THIRTY-EIGHT

CHARLIE

I walked through the streets of Sanctuary next to my mates. The pixies had insisted on keeping Karly and Isis for at least a couple of hours while Travis and Garrett promised to get me situated in their home. After seeing the smiles on the babies' faces, I'd been able to leave them... just for a few hours. The pixies had assured me they would bring the babies to us later that evening, along with all the equipment we would need to care for them.

A few hours to just be with Travis and Garrett were all I could think about right now. I wanted to be safely wrapped in their arms without fear of what was going to come jumping through the window next. At least for a few moments.

They said Sanctuary was safe. They'd reminded me about the barriers on the houses that snapped in and out of place each time a window or door was open, preventing Djinn from teleporting in and out. I knew several of the vampire Protectors that guarded the town, among the other very powerful residents.

Rose had gathered a veritable army of supernaturals, all to protect one small group of almost-human women. The ultimate prize that Xerxes still hadn't succeeded in taking back.

A deep, dark place in my consciousness liked that I would be a part of a group that kept Xerxes from something he desperately wanted. He should be made to feel frustration, pain, and loss, among many other emotions.

We turned a corner onto a street of small ranch-style homes. Green lawns and toys littered many front lawns, evidence of more children on the street. It would be nice for Isis and Karly to have playmates.

"This is ours." Travis pointed to the tan and red brick house on the left.

It was nice and clean. The lawn was trimmed.

I followed them up the porch steps and through the front door. The living room had a couch and a TV. There was no kitchen table in the dining area, only a couple of barstools shoved up against the bar in the kitchen. We walked through the galley kitchen, and I released a small sigh of relief—at least the sink was clear of dirty dishes.

"The bedrooms are through the living room. I'm in the master right now," Travis said. "But we'll set up the rooms however you want them."

"Shouldn't we all share a room?" I asked, puzzled by why he'd brought up sleeping arrangements.

"We weren't sure if you would want your own space," Garrett answered.

Some Lycan females demanded space to themselves, only sleeping with their mates when they chose. I was not one of those.

"I don't want you anywhere except in bed with me," I said.

Both men beamed, their mouths curving into smiles, and Garrett swooped me up first, pressing his lips against mine. It was gentle but insistent. I surrendered to the kiss, letting my body melt into his. Travis came up behind me, sandwiching me between them.

Garrett's tongue plunged into my mouth, tasting every inch. I wrapped my arms around his neck and pulled even closer. Travis' teeth grazed the back of my neck, and a shiver ran down my spine. My sex throbbed between my legs, and I wanted nothing more than their cocks inside me. Breathing turned to panting, and I moaned as Travis' hands fondled my breasts, rolling the erect nipples between his thumb and forefingers.

More. I hadn't realized how desperately I wanted them until I was standing at the foot of a bed with their hands and mouths all over me. Our clothes disappeared with a few tugs, and I wrapped my fingers around Garrett. He was ready for me, and I was ready for him. Travis' cock pressed against my backside, and I shivered, excitement warming my body. My skin tingled, and I panted for air between Garrett's kisses.

Travis' hands grabbed my hips and twisted me to face him. I transferred my arms to his neck and sighed as his mouth covered mine, taking over where Garrett had left me already breathless; Travis was determined to steal away what little air I managed to gasp for.

One of his hands dropped between our bodies and slid down my stomach, stopping with his fingers positioned over my throbbing mound. One digit delved deeper, finding the swollen clitoris and circling it ever so subtly.

Fire erupted within me, and I saw white. My orgasm writhed through my body and I dug my fingers into Travis' shoulders, letting my head drop backward.

Garrett palmed my neck and kissed my mouth, turning my head over my shoulder.

"Please," I begged. I needed to feel them. At least one, if not both.

"This is all about you, love," Travis growled in my ear and nipped at the earlobe. "Only you."

"B-but, I-I—" The words faded to a gasp. Travis sunk fingers inside me, while continuing to play with my clit using his thumb.

Garrett kissed and nibbled and kissed more. He bit my shoulder just hard enough to feel his teeth before continuing with his caresses down my back.

"To the shower first." Travis murmured. "Let us wash the horrors of the day away while we worship your body, Charlie."

Gods, that sounded perfect.

They half-carried me between them through their bedroom and into the large en suite bathroom. Before I could take a deep breath, my clothes were gone and all three of us were beneath a spray of heavenly, scalding hot water. The smoke, grass, and dirt washed down the drain. Garrett and Travis massaged soapy washcloths over every inch of my skin. Once I was clean, they switched from the cloths to trailing their mouths along the lines and curves of my breasts, my stomach, and up and down my arms.

Nerve endings fired under their attentions, and my legs threatened to give way. Hotness poured over my skin, but the true heat was between my legs. I needed to feel them inside me. My mind knew I was safe, but I needed to feel it.

"Move her to the bed," Garrett said, his voice raw and needy. The sound made the throb between my legs intensify.

"Damn, love, you are just melting under our touch." Travis slipped his hand between my legs and slid a finger between my slick folds. Too fast. I whimpered at the emptiness when he withdrew his finger.

A moment later, I was spread across the big bed, and Garrett's head was between my thighs. Travis' mouth attended to my pebbled nipples while he held my wandering hands tight above my head, giving me no ability to touch or caress them in return.

I raised my head and kissed along Travis' shoulder; the soapy freshness of his scent filled my lungs.

Garrett's mouth fell to my sex, and every muscle inside me tensed then relaxed as his tongue licked my clitoris and then plunged deep inside, mimicking the act I so desperately wanted them to follow through with.

I tried to ask again, but Travis' mouth fell to my nipples, cruelly bringing them back to painfully erect peaks. All ability to form coherent speech left my brain. Garrett had me at his mercy. They both did.

My eyes closed as I drifted into the place where orgasms lived. Garrett pulled away and replaced his tongue with his cock, driving home with one smooth movement. I sailed in the moment with him, flying higher with each drive until we shattered together with a shout.

Before I could come down from the ethereal place of bliss, they swapped places and Travis thrust, filling me again with a hard, needy cock. I clamped down as he pumped in and out, pushing me higher again, back into the space where only bliss existed. I came hard around him, and he shouted through his release as his body stiffened against mine.

Their seed filled me with soothing warmth. I turned on my side and pulled one of Travis' pillows against my chest and snuggled into the downy softness. Moving wasn't high on my list, and I hoped they would let me sleep, wrapped in the scent of our lovemaking.

"I love you, Charlotte. Sleep well," Garrett's voice crooned from above my head.

"We'll be back to check on you later, love." This time it was Travis' slightly deeper bass voice.

"I love you both," I murmured, burying my face in Travis' pillow.

Sweet release was mine.

CHAPTER
THIRTY-NINE

TRAVIS

She was here. In our house. My brother and I stood, watching her fall into a peaceful sleep. The tightness that had been present in my chest since her very first phone call released. We'd been ready to stay. To lead her pack with her.

"It's good to have her home," Garrett murmured.

I couldn't have spoken truer words.

"Yes, it is. Come on. Let's give her some time to sleep." He followed me out of the bedroom and closed the door softly behind him.

"Rose texted," he said. "The pixies have baby stuff."

My heart climbed into my throat. *Babies. What are we going to do with two babies?*

Garrett chuckled and patted me on the back. "Breathe, big guy. They're just little people. How hard can it be?"

"Which room do we put them in?"

"Mine," he said, sauntering down the hall as if this didn't faze him in the least.

I shook my head and followed him. We worked for a solid hour, moving his furniture to the garage, vacuuming the floors, scrubbing the windows. It was disgusting the layers of dirt that accumulated on something that probably hadn't been cleaned since we moved in.

Sweat beaded on my brow after everything was finished, and my t-shirt was damp down the length of my spine. I needed another shower and a few minutes to play a game. We'd salvaged an old game system, and Garrett's genius had gotten it running again. The Bateman gals had enchanted the TV so we could use it without the government tracking its location. Our living room was a very popular one on the block.

"What are they going to sleep in?" I asked, staring at the now-clean and very empty bedroom.

"Pixies are bringing it over. They should be here any minute."

"We don't need to help?"

"Did you not hear me say pixie? Have you never seen them move things?"

"I guess not," I growled, obviously missing something.

He threw up his hands in surrender. "Hey, you're the one who's lived here longer."

A small rap at the door signaled their arrival. I hurried through the hallway to the front and pulled open the door. Bella, with her sky blue hair, stood on the porch holding Isis in her arms, the bigger toddler... at least I was pretty sure the bigger one was Isis.

"Hey, big guy. Take her for me. Garrett said the

nursery was clear. We've got furniture to set up." She handed me the little girl, and I grabbed her under the arms, pulling her tight to my chest. She squirmed a little, and I rearranged her legs so they hung free instead of squashed up against me.

"Don't squeeze her so hard," Bella said before turning around and directing a train of... *Shit*... The furniture was floating. *Of course.* Garrett had known they would use pixie dust. No wonder he wasn't worried about helping.

"Move out of the way, hon." She poked my arm with one finger. "We've got a lot to do."

Several pixies followed her through, herding a baby crib and a miniature bed.

"Wait," Garrett said, joining me in the living room to watch the procession. "Won't she crawl out of that bed?"

"Probably," one of the pixies said, giggling as she and the bed floated down the hallway.

"Probably?" I hissed, "How's that going to work?"

"It's called training, hon," another pixie answered, following the bed down the hallway with Karly in her arms.

I hurried after her, careful not to jostle Isis. The toddler in my arms giggled and pointed to items floating through the house above our heads toward the empty room... well, it had been empty. There was a crib, a bed, a rocking chair, a dresser, and something I had no idea what to call with diapers stacked on the shelves. Another corner held a small bookshelf and *books*. A basket of brightly colored blocks and toys sat next to it.

"Where did those come from?" I asked.

Bella turned and smiled. "I asked Miles for a few

things from his library. Come on over here and let me tell you how everything works."

"Where did you get everything?"

"Storage. These aren't the first babies in town, you know," she answered. "Here's the changing station. Karly sleeps in the crib, but you'll have to train Isis to stay in her big girl bed. We bathed them for you already, too. So don't worry about that tonight."

The instructions went on and on. Things I'd never heard of. Schedules we needed to maintain. Foods they could and/or shouldn't eat.

I glanced at Garrett, and his eyes had the same glazed, overwhelmed expression I imagined in mine. One of the pixies handed him Karly, and then each of them kissed both of the little girls before they wished us good luck and left us standing in the middle of the room.

When the front door closed and the house was silent except for Garrett and my nervous heartbeats, I eyed him and frowned. "What the hell was that?"

"Hey!" he scowled. "Language, dude."

My eyebrows shot up, and for the first time in years, I felt heat creep into my cheeks.

"Sorry." I wasn't sure who I was apologizing to... him or the girls.

"Toys!" Isis squealed, pointing to the bucket filled with a variety of items. "Down. Down." She wriggled until I gave in. Once her feet hit the ground, she took off toward the bucket, sitting down and immediately dumping its contents all over the floor.

Karly copied the toddler, and Garrett regarded me with a questioning look. The baby yelled, and he quickly put her on the floor, as well. She tottered a few steps before dropping with a plop to her bottom. It didn't slow her down. Seconds later, she was crawling toward Isis.

"This isn't so hard," Garrett said, sitting down on the floor next to the girls and crossing his legs. He picked up a toy airplane and flew it around the air. Both girls clapped their hands and giggled.

I smiled. *Maybe we can do this.*

Only the gods knew I'd spoken to soon.

Isis got up a few minutes later and started walking around the room. She looked like she was inspecting the furniture at first, but then she went behind the rocking chair, and a very distinct smell hit my nostrils.

"Isis!" We both jumped up, and the toddler ran out from behind the chair.

Garrett caught her and held her body out away from his as she continued to scrunch up her legs and face. "Dude, she's still going!"

"What are you telling me for?" I pointed to the hallway. "Take her to the toilet."

He ran with her, holding her body away from his.

"Get in here and help me!" he shouted.

I glanced at Karly, who had watched the entire exchange silently, although I was quite sure there was a smile in her eyes that said we'd be doing the same thing with her momentarily. "Stay," I said, pointing at the toys.

Darting down the hall, I turned into the bathroom and saw Garrett holding Isis above the toilet.

"Take off her pants, man. I've only got two arms."

"Okay," I grabbed the toddler's shorts and tugged them off. The diaper was another matter.

"The tabs on the side. Bella said those were like Velcro," he advised, wrinkling his nose.

The smell was indeed getting worse. I pulled the tabs and removed the diaper. Poop rolled from inside it and hit the bathroom floor with an ominous *plop plop plop*. Everywhere but inside the toilet.

"By the gods!" Garrett shouted. "Couldn't you have at least directed it into the bowl?

A burst of female laughter from the hallway turned both our heads. Charlie was wrapped in my blue terry-cloth bathrobe and was expertly balancing Karly on a hip using only one arm. Her other arm was hanging onto the doorframe trying to keep herself from doubling over.

The laughter made her face turn red. She tried to speak, but no intelligible words came out before another roll of laughter took her over.

"I'm done," Isis said, kicking her legs in the air.

Garrett snorted. "You think!" He pushed her toward me, and I shook my head.

"What am I supposed to do?"

"Dude, you either clean her or clean the floor."

My eyes drifted to the formless brown globs on the bathroom floor and then back to the struggling toddler. I was less afraid of the shit.

"You keep her," I said.

All the while Charlie continued to laugh her ass off in the hallway, trying to talk but not having any breath to do so efficiently. Her humor wasn't annoying; the situation was probably that of a three-ring-circus in her opinion. Plus, just hearing her laugh instead of cry was worth cleaning up Isis' poop every day of the week. Although, I rather hoped it didn't become a habit.

Garrett groaned, but carefully stepped over a glob and exited the bathroom with the toddler held at arms' length from his body. I turned back to the floor and swallowed down the disgust rising from my gut. It smelled worse than a decomposing animal. What in the world did this child eat?

Once the bathroom floor was cleaned up, I joined them in the nursery, formerly Garrett's bedroom. It was hard to believe it'd had his things in it only a few hours ago. Now it was a baby kingdom.

"Use the wipes and hold her legs up with your other hand," Charlie's voice carried from across the room. She was hovering around the diaper table-thing. Isis was lying on top of it, and Garrett was doing his best to wrestle two weaving legs and clean her bum at the same time.

I chuckled and leaned against the doorframe. This was what life should be. Not fighting armies and crazy psychopathic lunatics. It should be about family and chasing a toddler about to poop in her diaper. These were the moments that started something new.

"Now fold the new diaper between her legs... yes... and use the tabs to hook it in place. Good!" She rubbed Garrett's arm, and I felt her pride in him over such a small thing. His excitement over the accomplishment flooded our bond with joy. Joy over success with a diaper.

"Down, down!" Isis squealed. Garrett lifted her from the table and set her on the floor. She ran back toward the toys wearing only a shirt and diaper.

"Her pants," Garrett said, his eyes wide with embarrassment for the child who didn't look like she had a care in the world.

"She's fine. I'll dress her later. Just let her play," Charlie said. She bent over and put Karly on the floor and watched her crawl back to the toy corner.

Garrett slid an arm around Charlie's waist and hugged her close. "Sorry we woke you."

"It was worth it," she answered, flashing him a smile and then me. She held out an arm, inviting me to join them.

I crossed the room and stood with them. "It was pretty funny, wasn't it?"

"My dear brave, wonderful mates, it was the funniest thing I've seen in my entire life." She leaned her head against my shoulder and sighed.

"What are we going to do when there's another?" Garrett asked, his voice carrying more than a little fear.

I swallowed. *Another one?*

"They'll equal us in numbers. And how do you hold one with one arm like you were doing? Is it even possible to hold both of them at once?" Garrett rapid-fired the questions.

Charlie moved her head from my shoulder to his and patted the front of his chest with her palm.

"I love you."

"But what about—"

"Shhhhh," she said, pressing a finger to his lips. "Just enjoy the moment."

I pressed a kiss to her temple and moved across the

room, sinking to the floor next to the two children. She was right.

Moments like these were for savoring.

Flashes where everything was good.

Everyone was safe and happy.

Everyone could feel the love in the room.

Isis crawled over onto my lap and leaned against my chest. She didn't say anything. She just was there with me, sharing the magick that flowed between us. Our mate bond was growing, expanding to include the children. It wrapped around each of us like a comforting blanket. Peaceful. Calm.

Charlie and Garrett sat down next to me, and Karly crawled into Garrett's lap and beamed up at him.

I met Charlie's gaze and smiled.

A perfect moment, no matter how fleeting, was still perfect when it happened.

I hope you enjoyed MY WARRIOR WOLVES!
Thank you for spending time with me in my world.
Please consider leaving a short review. Each one helps tremendously.
XOXO
Krystal Shannan

Turn the page to read part of book 6, MY GUARDIAN GRYPHON!

CHAPTER ONE

GRETCHEN

"What about this one," I asked, my voice filled with a hope he didn't notice. He never noticed. I could choose the most romantic story in the Blackmoor's enormous library, and he would still look at me like I was the eleven-year-old girl who'd asked him a random history question fifteen years ago.

His wide brow wrinkled over amber-colored eyes that shimmered with flecks of gold. He was a man women dreamed about. At least I dreamed about him.

Tall. Dark. Mysterious. Broad shoulders melted into a tapered waist and narrow hips. Muscles went on for miles, muscles that I wanted to touch and feel against my naked skin. My stomach clenched and rolled. Lower in my body, a steady hum and throb started, growing with the ache inside I felt every time we were together. It'd gotten worse with each passing year.

By the gods, Gretchen, get a hold of yourself.

"*Antony and Cleopatra*?" The inflection of his voice carried surprise, and the words were spaced out, like he'd had to stop and think between the names.

I glanced up from the time-aged book. Not surprised. Even from across the expansive room he could read the embossed gold title on the cover like it was only inches from his face—he had telescopes for eyes. He never missed anything.

Except what was right in front of him. I could probably wrap my naked body in a clear shower curtain and he'd still be oblivious.

"It's one of the most classical romances of that time period." I emphasized the word romance, hoping to lead his mind in that direction. I'd never give up. Even if it took my whole life to make him notice me.

"Cleopatra was a..." His voice sharpened, filled with an emotion I couldn't quite pin down. Irritation. Annoyance. Disbelief. "She was a smart woman, but she only loved herself. Both Caesar and Marc Antony fell for her wiles. Perhaps it did look like a love story from the outside, but from the inside, the only thing you could see was her cold, calculating heart." He sat on our favorite couch and watched me expectantly. I half-expected him to pat the seat cushion and call me over. But he didn't. He just sat there—waiting. Frustratingly patient and oblivious as ever.

Well, that didn't work. Stupid Cleopatra. Instead of associating her with romance, he's all bristled and annoyed. "So you're saying Shakespeare got the story wrong?" I flipped through the worn pages of the classic. The smell of aged, stale paper had long since become a staple. My life revolved around escaping my quarters in the basement level of the castle. The library had started out a childhood fascination with history—humans—and a way to escape the mundane tasks the Sisters were constantly participating in—gardening, meditating, learning how to copulate to encourage fertilization.

On and on and on.

I didn't get out of all the required studies, but I'd missed enough over the years that many of the Sisters were more than aware that I actively refused to participate in the destiny laid out for us thousands of years ago by the Lamassu—an ancient supernatural race more powerful than any other on Earth. A destiny that included giving myself to a stranger every weekend until I became pregnant. The House of Lamidae's sole purpose was to procreate to increase the power of our collective visions—visions that would lead us to the eight Protectors. Vampire warriors who Rose—the Lamassu Sentinel who'd been protecting our House for thousands of years—would use to fulfill the prophecy.

Bile rose in my throat, and I took a deep breath, willing it back down into my stomach where it belonged. I put a hand on the end of the bookshelf and exhaled. My stomach calmed, and the urge to vomit no longer waited anxiously behind my tongue.

"Are you unwell, Gretchen?" The concern in his voice gave light to my flickering hope. But I wanted more. More than just the concern of a friend.

"I'm fine," I answered, trying to purposefully sound more upbeat than I felt.

"You look a little green."

Seriously? I am not green. "I'm fine. Please read Cleopatra's story." Living in a town filled with ancient immortals had its perks. They'd experienced it. Breathed air with many of the people in the books I'd read over the years. "How well did you know her?"

"Not personally, but I heard much about her from others in her employ. It was difficult to live in that time and not know *about* her."

"You're better than any book in this library. You know that, right?"

He blinked, raising his eyebrows. His lips parted for a moment before he closed them again. Closed off the emotion he'd let slip through the armor he permanently wore.

"We're lucky the Blackmoor's saved what they did during the American Riots. Most of the books here are the only copies left in North America. Oral testimony will never compare with the written word."

"I know. I know. Supernaturals are the only ones who raced to save history while the American people just eradicated everything—knowledge, individuality, expression. You've reminded me many times." When I'd first come across Alek Melos relaxing in a corner of Miles and Eli Blackmoor's library, I'd desired nothing more than the truth—an answer to a single question about what had torn apart the United States. I'd gotten so much more.

He'd told me which stories were real and which stories weren't. What events had led to the downfall of one of the most powerful countries on Earth? So strange to think there were other worlds. Well—at least two. Earth and Veil.

Still, my mind wondered if there could be even more. I'd asked him once and he'd shrugged, saying he hadn't heard of any others.

"If you don't like discussing Cleopatra, I can pick something else." The stories used to be what drew me to the library day after day to learn everything I could from the quiet man I'd grown to care so deeply for. But now the stories were just the ancillary reason I went to the library. Now I desired something else completely.

I wanted to see Alek. Be next to him. Feel his touch. I wanted to belong to him. Something deep inside me sang every time we were in the same room. Joy filled me when we touched.

"It is a good tale. We should still read it."

"She committed suicide by snake. Was that real?" I walked across the room, enjoying the plushness of the Persian carpets covering the floor, and sank down onto the couch cushion next to Alek. The curtains on the floor-to-ceiling window behind us were drawn back with silken cords thicker than my wrists, and the afternoon light spilled in on my shoulders.

Alek's body, hard as the stone walls of this castle, burned hotter than the sunlight against the skin of my arm, but I leaned closer anyway. My mind automatically readied to receive the vision I always saw when I touched him, but I pushed it away this time.

Controlling my gift was something I'd mastered years ago. Some of the Sisters never learned to turn the switch on and off, but I had and took full advantage of not *seeing* things every time I touched someone or something. I pitied those of my sisters, who had to endure visions of past, present, and future any and every time they touched another being.

My past, present, and future was sitting right next to me. He just didn't know it yet, or if he did, he was doing a fine job of concealing it.

I crossed my legs on the silky brocade couch cushion and let my dress pool in the gap between them. The men who came to the castle for the *joinings* were always telling me my legs were long and beautiful, but I wanted Alek to notice them, not strangers there to ogle my body in hopes that I'd pick them for a *joining*.

Only Alek.

Only his hands would ever touch my body. That'd been my vow from the second I'd first had the vision of us together three years ago.

"She did," Alek answered. His rich, velvety bass tone drew me out of my bouncing thoughts. "She was to be captured. Taken prisoner. She was proud and cornered." His deep voice rumbled from the center of his chest, sending little fiery darts of joy straight to my nervous system. I loved listening to him speak.

These meetings in the library were the only thing that had kept me sane in this prison of stone through the last decade. Alek was my light. My hope. I still remembered the day I'd first met him, and it made me smile.

He pressed his lips together just slightly before speaking. "What are you thinking about?" His gaze bore into me, steady and strong, piercing straight through to my heart.

"The day I met you." I kept my tone soft, doing my best to hide the desire I knew would stream out of me like an overflowing bath if ever given the chance. "I remember wondering why people thought you were scary."

His eyes widened again. "You didn't find me frightening?" His mouth remained flat, but his dark brown eyes sparkled with amusement.

My destiny had been chosen for me the day I was

born. I wanted to tell him how much I hated it. How much more I wanted. I wanted to throw myself into his arms and tell him about my vision of us together. The perfect picture of the future that appeared to me every time I touched him.

"Never." I shook my head. "You were big and gruff, but you were kind. You took the time to answer the questions of a child who sought the truth. And you kept answering my questions. You keep teaching me, even now." I looked down to the carpet and breathed away the dampness in my eyes. I pressed my lips together and fought for control of my emotions. He made it look so easy, but it wasn't for me. My emotions leaked like sieve from inside to outside where everyone could see everything.

I'd forsaken all for the man who'd stolen my heart, and he didn't even know it. He had me. My whole heart. My mind. My everything would be his if only he…asked.

He cared for me. I knew he did.

I could feel it every time we spoke. Every time we touched. It could be so much more.

Everyone in the town watched out for me and the other Sisters of Lamidae. They protected us. Died for us. We were the chosen ones, the seers who needed to be shielded from everyone and everything. But Alek cared more. He had to. He spent so many hours with me—reading, talking, discussing things about his world I would never see. Because I would never be free from this castle.

"I'm glad our time together has been good. Reading with you is very… rewarding."

His words jarred me from my thoughts. *Rewarding?* I

wanted to scream that I loved him. Wanted to ask him how he could just sit by and let me battle Rose and the Sisters and everything around me. I wanted to ask him about that pause in his response, too. Had I missed something? Had he shown me affection in a way I'd missed?

But I didn't ask. I let it go.

The Sisters of Lamidae could see the future, and that was dangerous because people would use us to further their agendas—specifically Xerxes, Rose's brother-in-law, the only other Lamassu alive. He'd murdered his own brother and made it his mission in life to steal the Sisters from Rose. On and on the warnings rattled from the older Sisters. From Rose herself. We were too valuable to be allowed any rights, any freedom.

OUR ONLY DESTINY.

Have babies.

Build the numbers to strengthen the magick.

More magick meant better visions.

Better visions meant the prophecy would be fulfilled sooner and everyone would be safe from Xerxes foul intentions.

Fuck that.

We'd been on a mission to find the eight Protectors for thousands of years and still hadn't succeeded. Not that I could ever say any of that out loud. Everyone expected us to stay in line. Follow the rules. Fulfill our destiny.

It just wasn't working for me.

"You're going to catch a chill. Why aren't you wearing

a cloak?" His tone was matter-of-fact, not even the slightest bit suspicious or interested in why I'd worn a dress that showed ample cleavage or why I'd purposefully bared most of my legs.

I spread the skirt of my dress over my legs to cover them.

He took the book from my hands and met my gaze with his beautiful brown eyes. I loved the way flecks of gold danced in them when he was irritated. It was probably part of the reason I continually tried to rile him for one reason or another. Just to see the glint of the Gryphon within. The whole shifting animal sharing a soul thing was pretty damned interesting. I'd never seen him shift before, but asking him at some point had crossed my mind.

I kept my voice light and fun, and I returned his invasive stare with a bright smile. "You're my personal heater. The last thing I need when I'm with you is a cloak." I couldn't help the laugh that rose inside me. I loved that he called a sweater or cover-up a cloak, so old-fashioned. I'd never seen anyone in Sanctuary wear an actual *cloak*, but I didn't get out much. Alek said people rarely wore them anymore.

Cloaks were from the old books we read, old stories of times so different from what existed now. At least that's what he told me. I had to take his word for it, having never set foot outside the castle walls.

Alek shook his head ever so slightly, amused again, but still no show of emotion.

I didn't get him to smile or laugh often, but it was worth it to try. His laugh made my insides melt and my stomach do a somersault. And his smile...*Damn*. There wasn't another man in town with a smile as perfect as Alek's. A smile that filled the void in my soul.

He opened the book and began reading the opening to Shakespeare's *Antony and Cleopatra*. His accent morphed after the first few lines. Listening to him read Shakespeare was heaven. The lilt of his voice as he read the words from the page was enchanting. Like a vision, it carried me away into the story, blocking out all reality. Blocking out the situation I had facing me again tonight.

Suitors.

Men came to the castle every weekend. Men approved and vetted and offering themselves to the Sisters of Lamidae in exchange for a night of mutual pleasure—called *joinings*. A night they would not remember after they left. It was all part of the contract.

They knew their memories would be wiped, and yet they still agreed. We were an experience they couldn't get anywhere else. A lot of the men came back multiple times, and the same Sister would take him to her bed week after week, month after month—a twisted way of pretending they had a relationship with their sperm donor.

Even though the men didn't remember.

We did.

It may have been a one-sided relationship, but it worked for many. Some Sisters didn't care and chose a new bed partner each time they were ready to conceive again. We were asked to have at least two children during our lifespan, but many Sisters found refuge in having many children—at least the ones who could manage it. It filled their days with happiness and laughter to have baby after baby.

While others viewed it as I did—cursing a new generation into exile and a lonely existence. And then there were those who were never able to conceive. Through the years, more and more of the Sisters were plagued by infertility—or the men they chose were the culprits. No one really knew for sure.

Choosing a man to lie with over and over again until we had our minimum of two children was required. One might say it was ingrained in us by something so powerful that it consumed our every thought. We didn't just need to have children. We would lose our minds if we didn't. Several Sisters, who were never able to conceive, fell into a deep depression, ultimately taking their lives. A fine display of magick gone terribly wrong.

There always had to be a new generation of Sisters. Our power would deplete if our numbers got too low. They were too low right now.

It was our destiny. My destiny. One that I refused to accept, regardless of the burning agony deep in my gut that demanded I conceive.

But the child I wanted...the relationship I wanted... was a dream I'd never be allowed to make reality. Playing in the dungeon of the castle was permitted with the supernatural citizens of Sanctuary as long as no penetration was involved. Many of my Sisters enjoyed a little kink—or a lot, especially the ones who were hopelessly childless. Their fascination for play was just a way to distract them from the pain and depression that haunted them every month when their cycle started yet again—reminding them of their barrenness.

But *playing* was a pastime, not a path to children. We weren't allowed to have children with a supernatural. It was genetically impossible.

Or so Rose said.

It made logical sense in a way. Most supernatural species could only have children with their species. Though there were a few that could cross the genetic barrier—Lamassu being one—it was not common. At least from what I'd overheard through the years.

I leaned my cheek against Alek's strong arm. The rise and fall in his voice carried my imagination into the lyrical lines of Shakespeare. Everything fell away. All the worry and concern about tonight. None of it mattered. I wouldn't be forced to choose a suitor. Not today, perhaps not for many more months. I was only twenty-six, still plenty of childbearing years ahead of me, but the time was coming. I knew I wouldn't be able to avoid making a choice much longer.

A fight I would eventually lose. Depression gripped my soul, and I turned my focus back to the beautiful drama Alek was performing for me. I should be enjoying the moment, not dreading the coming night.

He reached the end of the first act and closed the book.

"I know this is just a story, but have you known anyone who loved the way Shakespeare describes?" I gazed up at him, and he rewarded me with a quick nod. No smile, though. Gods, I wanted a smile. *Please.* It'd been over a week since I'd coaxed one out of him.

"Miles, Eli, and Diana love with the same fierceness Shakespeare attributes to Antony and Cleopatra. Erick and Bailey. Killían and Eira. Charlie and her two mates, Travis and Garrett. There are many who I've met through the millennia who love and have loved in the way the great storyteller describes."

"Have you?" I asked bravely, wanting desperately to know. A part of me needed to know if he pined for a lost love or if the man was truly oblivious to every signal I'd attempted to hurl in his direction.

"No."

That's it? That's all he was giving me, a flat single-syllabled *no*? Not that I wasn't selfishly glad. I wanted his love for myself. I didn't want to compete with some ethereal memory of a woman who'd left him or died. "So you still have that to look forward to," I whispered without thinking.

The second the words had tumbled from my lips, terror tightened my lungs and I waited for a response that said I'd gone too far or crossed a line I shouldn't have.

He handed the book to me, then tilted his head, and kissed the top of mine. His lips were so soft and caring, perfection-embodied, but I didn't want the you're-a-sweet-child-who-I-like-to-tell-stories-to kiss. I wanted the kiss to be on my lips, and I wanted it to say you're-mine-and-I-can't-imagine-living-another-day-on-earth-without-you.

Alek was that for me already.

"I should go. The castle begins its rumbling for the start of the weekend's festivities." His tone had taken on the caretaker vibe, the one that dismissed me from his presence. But I wasn't ready to leave. Not yet. And I didn't give a flying fairy's ass about the so-called festivities tonight.

"We have plenty of time. I don't have to go." I circled my arm around his and snuggled closer to his side, reveling in the heat and hardness of his body. Thoughts of running my hand along his chest to feel the strength beneath the soft jersey t-shirt he wore flickered across the stage of my imagination, along with the vision of our bodies, naked and entwined on a bed.

I wanted more from the life I'd been born into. And one day I was going to get it. Happiness waited for me each time I touched him. Eight seconds of bliss. Eight seconds of Alek and me lying in a bed together, smiling and laughing and in love. In the vision, he would kiss my stomach and whisper endearments to the child I was carrying. Our child.

We would have a child. That's why I didn't fear the sadness and depression that typically found the childless Sisters.

I would have a child. His child.

He was my beast—my Gryphon warrior.

He had always been mine. And I would be his.

Sign up for Krystal's VIP mailing list for access to lots of exclusive not-for-sale-anywhere stories, free books and more.
www.krystalshannan.com/newsletter/

~ Join Shannan's Sanctuary ~

Follow and/or **Subscribe** to **exclusive** bonus stories, preview my new books as I write, have LIVE chats with me, and and more on my Patreon channel! I can't wait to get to know you better!

www.patreon.com/krystalshannan

ALSO BY KRYSTAL SHANNAN

FOR A FULL LIST PLEASE GO TO KRYSTALSHANNAN.COM/BOOKS

Sanctuary, Texas
Paranormal Romance
Completed Series

Sanctuary, Texas will take you on a heart-pounding-toe-curling ride into a town of fantastical creatures and a war for world domination you won't soon forget. The series has fated mates, growly heroes with soft spots for their strong spunky heroines, and enough spicy romance to make you blush. Don't miss this sexy, gritty, paranormal fantasy romance with a twist of darkness. There's a "big bad" you will love to hate and an amazing cast of characters across the series that build a family you won't want to leave behind.

Soulmate Shifters in Mystery, Alaska
Paranormal Shifter Romance

Winter in Mystery, Alaska just got a whole lot hotter. Dragon shifters, lions, and tigers oh my! When the Reylean's world burns, the Tribal survivors find themselves transported to earth through a magickal portal. This series has fated mates, and alpha heroes that will do anything to protect and pleasure and love their women. Come with them on a journey of fitting in, building a new Tribe, and finding out that true family is about more than bloodlines.

VonBrandt Wolf Pack
Paranormal Shifter Romance

Interested in tall, dark, and sexy cowboy wolf shifters? Somewhere, Texas is your town. The VonBrandt Wolf Pack will check every box for you--Stetson-wearing ranchers who can shift into wolves, Fated Mates, and enough high-adrenaline-action to make Bruce Willis shout with glee. Join the VonBrandt men as they win the hearts of the women they love and build a family that will give you all the warm and fuzzies.

Moonbound Wolves
Paranormal Shifter Romance
Completed Series

High octane action builds in this sexy wolf shifter series! A spin-off from the VonBrandt Wolf Pack Series. Follow the enforcers from the Somewhere, TX wolf pack as they uncover a sinister evil that threatens magick as they know it. Each of the seven books offers a happily ever after for a fated mate pair and will propel you into the next leg of the group's across-the-globe mission. Sexy cowboy werewolves and the mates they can't live without, meddling witches, and conspiracies abound in this action-packed paranormal romance series you won't want to miss.

Vegas Mates

Paranormal Shifter Romance

Completed Series

A high-paced series with fated wolf mates fighting to save the people they love. Jump on this roller coaster with sexy shifter men who will go through any trial and women who will stand at their side fangs bared. Follow the Demakis shifter sisters on their journey through their past and how it's affecting their future. Along the way they discover there's so much more to the legends about their wolves than their parents ever let on.

Bad Boys, Billionaires & Bachelors

Contemporary Romance

These three billionaire brothers from small-town Somewhere, TX will warm your hearts and make your toes curl all on the same page. The Stinson men are in a pickle. Good old grandpa put a clause in the will that says they can't inherit the family railroad business unless they get married and have a baby on the way in less than a year. Laugh and cry your way through their antics as they try to figure out how to open their hearts and their homes to women that take them totally by surprise! The sexy and emotional romps continue with more Somewhere, TX bachelors and bad boys!

Pool of Souls

Fantasy Romance

A little matchmaking in my life.

A little bit of Aphrodite by my side.

Jump into a fantasy-laden romance between the human souls the Goddess of Love is matching and Aphrodite's own romantic relationship with Ares, the God of War. It's a two-for-one special! And between the shenanigans on earth and the ones on Olympus, it's all sexy drama all the time.

ABOUT THE AUTHOR

USA Today Bestselling Author Krystal Shannan lives in a sprawling ranch style home with her husband, teenage son, and two almost teenage daughters. Her home is full of love and laughter and lots of animals. In fact the welcome mat warns visitors that it's a zoo inside—chickens, rabbits, rats, guinea pigs, dogs and fish! You name it, they've probably had it in their home at some point.

Krystal writes stories filled with magick, fantasy, passion, and just enough humor to make you laugh out loud. Join the fun and escape to a whole new world.

You can find me at www.krystalshannan.com and

subscribe to my newsletter for new release updates, but there's way more fun stuff on Patreon. Just sayin' :-)

— Hugs, Krystal

- patreon.com/krystalshannan
- amazon.com/author/krystalshannan
- bookbub.com/authors/krystal-shannan
- goodreads.com/KrystalShannan
- facebook.com/KrystalShannan

Made in the USA
Middletown, DE
18 March 2025